B L U R R

TYESHIA GAINER

BLURR

DEDICATION

I dedicate this book to two individuals — first my grandmother who I admire and who took responsibility to raise me. Without her, I wouldn't be the woman I was destined to be. Thank you, ma, for standing by my side and believing in me. You made a lot of this happen, and I can't thank you enough. I appreciate you more than anything. Love always your daughter.

The second person is my brother Tyrone (Rico). I want to thank you for believing in me and pushing me through this journey. Only you could understand the vision I was able to accomplish. Rico, you were more excited for me than I was for myself. You were the first person I told about the book and the first person who was able to see the vision from beginning to end.

Tyrone, you are a person who is honest. That's why your feedback was so essential, and meant so much to me. I was proud of myself for having you curious to know certain parts of the book and asking questions. That's how I knew it was good. Thank you for standing by my side and supporting me.

I know the both of you are proud of me and happy that I was able to accomplish my goal and many more things throughout my life. This is not the end, I promise it just the beginning.

Thank you! You mean so much to me. Love you

ACKNOWLEDGMENTS

I strove for a goal that I was able to accomplish. It took me four years to publish BLURR, but throughout the four years, I succeeded. Even though the tears, long nights and doubts, I managed to pursue a dream that became a reality. My family, friends and loved ones I know they are proud of me. Thanks for your support!

I want to thank you God for everything you have done. God you've blessed me in so many ways I can't thank you enough. Mainly by giving me a talent, I was able to utilize and excel in. I want to thank you for pushing me and blessing me with so much. You have given me so much to pursue, and I know this is not the end but the beginning of a new journey. Thank you, my God, and I will continue to walk by faith and not by sight. Love you so much. Amen.

To my grandmother, mother and best friend Audrey Gainer. Audrey you are a role model in my life. I call her G-ma because she can put up a fight. During the four years of writing BLURR, I had to battle with you fighting cancer. Blurr was able to distract me from what I had to witness. I was able to finish the book during the time of tears. I want to thank you, Grandma, because together we were able to stay strong and fight the battle. I love you more than you.

To my brother Tyrone (Rico). During the four years, Rico you were my biggest supporter and made sure I was able to accomplish this goal. I want to thank you, Rico, for believing in me when I almost gave up. I appreciate you for being my biggest fan! Love you so much.

As for my Aunts: Renee Gainer, Gail Gainer, Raquel Walker, Gloria Lee, Bernadette Thomas, Leona Johnson, Lisa Johnson, Tiffany Jones, Cora O'garro, and Jamella Martin. I know you ladies weren't aware of me writing this book and thinking when did I have the time. Well, ladies, this was a project I was working on, and it was not my intention not to share the great news, but I just wanted to complete the goal.

My aunts have been around for me throughout my 29 years — Aunt Raquel, Gloria, Bernadette, Leona Lisa, Cora, and Jamella. I want to thank you, ladies, for being strong black women. Each of you ladies have touched me differently and inspired me to become all that I could be. Thank you, and I love you.

As for Renee, and Gail, I want to thank you both for being fantastic aunts, sisters, and mother figures to me. I appreciate you, ladies, more than anything. God made it possible for me to become your younger sister. I love you ladies and Thank you.

To my Aunt Tonya Lucas, I want to say I am proud of you. You became one of my most influential role models — a woman who always was positive, spiritual and most of all TOUGH. I want to thank you because you showed me the value of real life. You inspired me to finish my book and also pushed me to complete my goal. Thank you for everything because you made me open my eyes and not complain about life. I understand why you published your book "This is my story." RIP to you. You will always be my Angel. Love you always. (PLEASE PURCHASE "THIS IS MY STORY").

As for my Cousins: Demone (Colee) Gainer, Parris (Gams) Cole, Audrey aka (NEACE) Gainer, Savion Gainer, Isaiah Gainer, Kurita (Tee-Tee) Gaskin, Shanaye aka (NAY NAY) Thomas, Bria Thomas, Tamar Johnson, Najah Gainer, Milrah Sercey, Darren (Peter pumpkin) Prince, Aszina Brister, Alena Brister, Rita Brister, Jay Cole, Vic, Thauna,

Tornia, Gina, and Akeem Gaskin. I know you guys are proud of me and also is my biggest fan. I want you guys to read my book and not look at me as a cousin, but as an Author. I want feedback and critique from you all. I knew if I spoke about the book, you guys would want me to tell you all about it. I already know you will support me and have my back on this project. So, thank you guys and love you, cousins.

To Demone, Parris, Neace, Savion, and Isaiah, we grew up to become more than cousins but sister and brothers. I know you guys will support me and enjoy this Journey as time goes on. I love you guys more than you even know it.

To my sisters and brother, Tyshana Gainer, Tyquasia and Shawn (Bucci). I hope this book inspires you and will inspire you guys to go after your dreams. I also know that you are proud of me and big supporters as well. Love you so much.

To my Nieces, Nephews and baby cousins, Tyleah Gainer, Aszaria Gainer, Genesis Walker, Aylila Johnson, and Messiah Walker. My Lil babies Savion (lil say) Gainer, Noah Gainer, Skylar Gainer, Baby Carter Gainer, Denim Gainer, King Cole, Tyonna, Xzavier, Millie, Aniyah Turner, Hezekiah Gaskin, Nyla Martin, Nya Martin, Samirah, and Kaleah. I love you guys so much, you are always on my mind and heart. As each of you gets older, I hope I inspire you guys to go after your dreams, and believe nothing is impossible. Love you always.

As for Aszaria, Tyleah, and Gen, I also hope I inspire you ladies to go after your dreams and hope you follow the ideas you want to pursue. Just know you can achieve many goals and become what you are destined to be. Love yall very much.

As for my other grandmothers, how can I forget about you ladies? Grandma Diane Gainer and Grandma Nacey (Nan) Thomas. I want to thank you, ladies, because you are very important in my life. I was able to hold a special bond between both of you, and no one will ever understand. Just know that I love you both very much and I know you ladies are proud of me.

To my Harlem family: The Canty's, Aunt Yvonne, Roxanne, Paula, Michelle, Monique, Mikey, Nacey, Corey, Jared, Jordan, Stephanie, Nakia, Uncle Fulton, Dwayne, and Brianna. I know you guys are proud of me especially you Paula. Paula, you were another person who I spoke to about my book. You know I couldn't forget to give you a shout out. Love you guys.

To the Bennerman family, I know you guys are proud of me. I couldn't forget to give you a shout out. Especially to Linda, Tisha, Jessica, Monette, Tiffany Aunt Sheron, and annoying Junior. My babies Iyana (ya-ya), Skylar, Jabril, Trayvon (tray-tray) Landen, Grayson, Tiyana, and Stephen. I love you guys. (See Linda I can't forget about you).

As for my uncles: Roland Gainer, I-True, and Gregg Walker. Each of you men gave me advice and support. You may not know how special you are to me, but you guys are very special to me. You became big brother of mine, and I know you are proud of me. Thank you, guys. Love you as well.

I can't forget to Shout out The Ogarro's family Najah Ogarro's, and Grandma Susie. Love you ladies.

Also want to give thanks to SOKETAHS, and Shic, Keisha & Sonya. Couldn't forget about you ladies. Love you ladies.

As for my friends/family, where to do I begin. Throughout the years I have lost and gained friends. Many people do not value friendship or know the meaning of true friendship especially when it comes to Loyalty. As for B.O(prince), Ms. T, Kiana Jones, Allante, Shardasia Mickens, Lashamecca Watson (mecca, she hates when I call her that) Danielle Sharne, James (Irv) Tinsley, Rara Brown, Kashaif Brown, Shameeka Wilson, Jovanna Briggs, and Ms. Linda. I want to thank you guys because you have been true friends to me. It's sad that you guys knew me very well and stayed by myself. Never hate or shade in your blood but pure love. I know you guys are proud of me and thanks for the support. Love Ya.

I can't forget my Post office family/friends: Mrs. Dionne Kelly, Mr. Derrick Hall, Mr. Ron Foreman, Devon Archor, Ariel Gonzalez, Kimberly Coburn, Mr. Farod, Mr. Anthony Rivera and many more. I appreciate you guys more than know. You guys have guided me and lead me in the right direction. You have also developed me to be a great BOSS. Especially to Mrs. Dionne; you became such an influential person in my life. I appreciate you more than you even know. Love you guys.

As for Pastor Sawyer and my church family NLM. Thank you, guys. I know you are proud of me and I couldn't forget to shout you out. However, I appreciate you guys. Especially for the support in my life. For my Pastor, you were always a big supporter in my life, especially in giving me advice. I will always love my NLM family.

I want to thank my editor Torey Warren. I appreciate the time you took out to support me on this project. You were such a big help, and I appreciate everything you have done. You were able to understand my vision and take the time out to assist me on my project. Torey, you made it possible to build up my confidence to complete another project. You were a real supporter.

I look forward to working with you in the future. Thank you so much, and you are another brother gained.

I want to Thank Lance Buckley, my book designer. I gave you a vision, that you were able to understand and execute. Thank you for taking the time out for my book cover, and I look forward to working with you in the future.

Last but not least. I never forget where I came from and where I grew up at — the place that never sleeps. I can't forget to shout out the whole Brooklyn, Fort Greene Projects (Farside).

I want to thank everyone for supporting me and hope you Enjoy! BLURR.

In Loving Memory of Uncle Derrick Gainer
In Loving Memory of Father Tyrone Gainer
In Loving Memory of Grandfather Roy Gainer
In Loving Memory of Aunt Tonya Lucus
In Loving Memory of my brother S.T (STUDD)

Always love...
Never forgotten...
Forever missed...
Always in my heart...

PROLOGUE

New Year's Eve party goes badly with deadly killing…

"Last Night there was a New Year's Eve party at Dumbo Lounge located in Brooklyn. A gentleman was bringing in the New Year celebrating his 28th birthday. There was a disagreement between two gentlemen and their group of friends. One witness stated, it started from a bump to the shoulder that escalated into an argument, then a fist fight. Another witness reported one of the gentlemen had apologized for bumping into the other gentlemen, but that gentlemen would not accept the apology.

Between both of the parties, they were being aggressive and threatening towards one another. Different parties of friends tried breaking up the argument, and it escalated again inside, causing a loud commotion. At this time both parties were fighting one another, creating a big brawl between the two.

Police arrived on the scene and broke up the brawl. There was a female shot and wounded in her lower back, and a man pronounced dead on the scene. The man suffered from internal bleeding from a gunshot wound to the chest and stomach.

The police did arrest a suspect at the scene, whom witnesses stated was the one who did the shooting. Police also arrested a group of people who were a part of the brawl that took place inside. An investigation is still on going, but the shooter will be charged with murder and attempted murder.

There are more investigations into the shooter, as well as the individuals of the party taken into custody. Names will not be revealed yet, until further investigation. Dumbo Lounge will be under investigation and remain a crime scene, until further investigation as well.

Family, friends and loved ones are supporting one another at the scene of this tragic event. Many are still shocked that this has happened and are in utter disbelief. We hope this crime is solved and the police are able to get to the bottom of this brawl, that resulted in two shootings.

There will be more on this investigation and updated information soon. Reporting Live on Eye Witness News...

CHAPTER 1

"**H**appy Birthday to you…. Happy Birthday too youuu… Happy Birthday to my babeeee… Happy Birthday, toooo you…Now make a wish, I said as I entered the room with 28 candles lit, causing his eyes to open, while lifting up with a grin. I climbed on top of him with the cake still in both hands. "Baby blow out your candles," I said smiling. Without a word, he blew the candles out. "What did you wish for?" I asked placing the cake on the nightstand, beside him. "I wished for you," he said pulling me over to lay on my back.

He reached over and kissed me on my lips. "Thank you, babe," he said reaching over giving me another kiss. "Eat your cake, I worked hard on this strawberry cake," I said. I had baked him a strawberry cake, with vanilla frosting and strawberry filling inside, just like he liked it. He turned over and wiped some icing with his finger and put it in my mouth. I licked it off his finger and kissed all over his hands, leading to his lips.

I could tell what we were leading up to. Leading into us making love and our bodies intertwined with one another. However, I couldn't resist the sensation he was taking me to. It was a feeling we both enjoyed. Ra had me losing my mind. I was feeling like another person inside and out. I couldn't help but want more of what he had to offer.

e kissed my body slowly, I rubbed every inch of his body
y with my finger.

"Babe let's eat," I said. I had made him a birthday dinner, which I knew he would enjoy. I whined, wanting him to stop but I couldn't resist the incredible feeling. The more he teased my body, the more I wanted more. He ignored my comment and continued to explore my body as I followed his lead. All Ra had on his mind was birthday sex.

Before I knew it, I'd climaxed on him not realizing my surroundings in that moment. Just when I thought we were finished, he turned me over and started kissing my back. He kissed and licked down my back sending chills up my spine.

I can't explain what caused me to react in that manner. The sensation of his actions caused me to lose control of myself. I forgot my thoughts, touch and everything else when he touched my body. It was like Ra was inside of me and controlling every part of me like a puppet master. All I could do was moan aloud in ecstasy. I was lying on my stomach with him lying on his back. I turned over and licked his forehead. "That was good babe", I said, giving him the eyes. We laid there for a second, still trying to recover from our arousal. I felt relieved and satisfied.

"Now can we eat?" I asked him, lifting up with my back against the headboard. "Nah, give me a piece of that cake," he said causing me to laugh. "You always must have your way," I said, with him looking at me from the corner of his eye. I reached behind the bed and grabbed for a box, slowly pulling it from behind my back. He took his last piece of cake and stuffed it in his mouth. I then sat the box on his chest, licking the frosting off his hand; as he picked up the box.

"What's this?" he asked looking at me. "Well open it and see what it is," I said smiling. He handed the box back to me, "No thank you" he said. My mouth widened "Babe come on, that's so rude," I said, crossing my arms over my chest. "I told you I don't want a gift from you, I'm good," he said.

Ra didn't like taking gifts from me. He always turned my gifts away. I'd end up having to take them back or they'd never be returned. I always appreciated him for just accepting me as I am and not taking advantage of me.

"Ra I know you don't like accepting my gifts, but take it this time. I promise I will never buy you anything again". However, deep down he knew I was lying. He still refused to open the box though. "I think you deserve something from me," I said, trying to change his mind. You've been so supportive of me completing school and graduating with my Masters, I had to give you something special." I said, expressing my feelings so he would reconsider. He looked down at the box and without a word he opened it. I stared at his face, keeping my fingers crossed, hoping he loved it.

To my surprise, his mouth widened and jaw dropped, while looking back and forth between me and his gift. I smiled because I knew he would like his gift. There laid a 18k white gold, Rolex GMT Master II watch, with brilliant, round cut diamonds. It glittered with a fiery radiance, engraved with the initials (RT) on the wristband.

"Damn Babe! It's beautiful. I LOVE this watch," he said, putting the watch on his left wrist. He examined it meticulously, while modeling it on his wrist. "Thank you, babe," Ra said with excitement. "You do huh?", I asked, "I knew you would, I planned this for months. I knew this would be perfect for you" I said.

"Yes, this is perfect," he said, "But you know you are better," he said, reaching over kissing me. Ra placed the watch back into the box and put it in the drawer that was beside him.

"Can we eat now?" I asked, getting up from the bed, as he grabbed me back, turning me over towards him. "Come on Ra let's eat! "I demanded". "I made your favorite dinner" I said, whining. "Oh yeah, and what's that?" he asked as he held me in his arms tickling me. "Mac& Cheese, Turkey Wings, Sweet potatoes, and Collard greens," I said, while squirming in his arms. However, he ignored what I was saying and kissed all over my face. "Babe…" I said to get his attention, but Ra continued to do what he wanted to do.

I knew he wanted round 2 so I whispered "I guess we can eat later". We entered into another world where sensation kept us alive. More like being hypnotized by a person you can feel inside and out. "Welcome to the world of a blissful blurr."

CHAPTER 2

I turned over to roses in my face and noticed Ra was not by my side. There lay dozens of red roses all over the bed, and a red bow ribbon attached. As I lifted up to smell the roses, I noticed the red ribbon trailed from the bedroom to outside the room. I pulled the cover from my naked body and went to the closet to put on my silk robe. I followed the red ribbon that trailed throughout the house into the living room.

It was a moment where you picture yourself in a movie. A piano sat in front of the window, where you could see the view of the city. It was picture-perfect. I saw a card and two boxes, so I opened up the boxes first, then read the cards later. It was so beautiful how he had set up everything.

Ra was always romantic. He would do everything to make moments like this memorable. Especially when it is my birthday. I picked up the smallest box first. There sat 18k diamond earrings, which were silver and gold. "Babe!" I said to myself. Even though he was not in my presence, I still brought up his name in excitement. They were so beautiful. I examined the earrings that sparkled as I turned the box. I placed the studs towards my ear and saw the reflection of them through the piano.

Next, I opened the second box. To my surprise, laid an Oyster 29mm, ever rose gold and diamond Rolex. "Wow! It's so beautiful," I pulled the watch out of the box. The bracelet part was diamond set pearl master and rounded five-piece links. White mother of pearl is what they called it and exposed it a pink and gold color lotus flower.

I was so deeply in love with this watch. Of course on the bracelet part, engraved was our initials (RT). I was in love. Aww baby, I thought smiling because he brought me the same gift, I got him.

Ra always shared his birthday with me. He would buy me a gift on his birthday every year without fail. When it's my birthday, he just showers me with gifts. However, most of the time I told him I didn't want any gifts, and of course, he ignored me. Ra was one of a kind. It was hard to find a man like him. He was a different kind of guy. Ra thought differently and lived differently. He owned his own construction business, and graduated with a Master's Degree in Architecture. Ra was an astute person who took pride in what he did.

Ra always helped people he cared about and gave advice. He gave back to his community, with new recreation centers for children and teens, for after-school programs. He also helped manage a basketball, baseball and football team. Ra was well known for his popularity and kindness. He was also highly respected, and considered an all-around fun, loving guy.

I must admit, Ra did have another side though. I did catch Ra cheating on me more than a couple of times, but I never left. I wasn't the type to go through his phone nor follow him to see if he was cheating. However, I knew he had cheated. It was just a woman's intuition that I could tell. I didn't throw shade towards him or bring it up in conversation though.

Don't get me wrong, we did have arguments that were so extreme, almost to the point of giving up. However, for some reason, I always found my way back to him. Ra knew I found out about some of the affairs, but I knew if I ever brought it up to him, it would hurt him more than it would bother me.

Ra always showed nothing but love towards me. He never disrespected me in my face to where I was blinded. He always respected me in my presence. I can admit he treated me the way a woman needs to be, but he needed to change. You can't change a man, he has to change for himself. Ra was not perfect, but he was perfect in my eyes, and I was over the top in love with him. My phone rang, interrupting my thoughts.

"Hello…" I answered

"Hey girl, you like the roses?" he asked, and I could tell he had that smirk on his face.

"Yes, thank you babe, for everything, especially my matching Rolex…" I said, smiling into the phone.

"Hahaha…" he was cracking up on the phone.

"You knew I got you that Rolex?" I asked

"Duh… I knew you purchased it because Joe told me" he said

Joe was the jewelry guy that Ra would purchase his jewelry from. It was a spot located in New Jersey, that had the best jewelry around.

"I knew Joe could never keep a secret, "I said to Ra.

"Girl you not low, I know everything, "Ra said joking.

" Whatever…Where you at?" I asked

"Oh, I had to take care of something," he said. However, I knew that must have been another excuse to escape to see one of his girls.

"Oh-ok," I said rolling my eyes. "What time are you going to be ready?" he asked.

"I'm not sure, I'm just waking up," I said

"Oh yeah, the food was slamming," he said. "Oh yeah, you finally ate," I asked smirking.

"Yeah baby, you were sleeping so peacefully I didn't want to wake you." he said.

"Is that right?" I asked

"Yeah after what I put on you… you couldn't handle it," he said laughing.

"Boy please," I said, shaking my head.

"Well be ready soon, I'll pick you up later," he said. *"Ok, later Hun,"* I said, and we hung up.

After hanging up the phone, I took another look at the watch and smiled. I placed it back into the box and grabbed the earring box, watch box and cards, and brought them into the room.

It was Ra's party tonight, that I'd been planning for a couple of months for him and it had to be perfect. I had just graduated with my Master's Degree in Management. I also received my Bachelor's Degree in Fashion Retail Management, and studied to be a coordinator for events. I wanted to also be an Event planner for weddings, parties, and much more. I loved doing designs and remodeling. It was a goal I wanted to pursue and wanted to start my own business by next year.

It would be the first project I actually worked on and I knew it had to be a masterpiece. Ra didn't mind me giving him a party, because it was the start of a New Year and his birthday. It was an exciting task for me to complete, as well as a hard project to achieve when trying to finish school.

Ra's party was at Dumbo Lounge in Brooklyn, under the Manhattan Bridge. It was a Masquerade party that I thought would be nice, bringing in the New Year. I chose the theme for this particular event because it represented a new face for the year, and a fresh start. (Out with the old in with the New).

Another reason why I chose this theme, was that one of our good friends was proposing when the ball dropped. Kareem and Kim were good friends of Ra and me. It was going to be a night to remember.

CHAPTER 3

I decorated the place fabulously, with a big ball placed in the center of the room. I planned as the ball dropped, to have party mixers that were silver and black burst out like an explosion. I also had a red carpet from the front entrance to the back of the lounge, where there were had two red velvet and gold chairs.

One chair was for Ra, and the other was for me. I was the queen of the ball, and of course, Ra was the king. We were going to be seated towards the back where we could watch the setting. On each side of us were two other chairs, that were for friends of Ra and me. Our friends were also going to be part of the setting for the Kings and Queens.

As for my centerpieces. I made Metallic Gold, glittery Wine bottles, that had ostrich feathers coming out of them. I also made different gold and shimmery black mask, that would be on each table. The gold and black masks were another part of the centerpieces.

I hired decorators to decorate the place as I wanted. I sketched out a design and formatted everything to be as I visualized. This way I did not have to rushed and have to set everything up myself. I could just relax and not worry about anything. I had hired servers to serve during the party, who would serve beverages. I also hired two photographers to take pictures for the night. One photographer was for outside, where he would snap photos before anyone entered;

while the second photographer was inside. It was a good theme, and I believed it would be the talk of the year.

I took a nice hot bath to comfort my body and to relax my mind. I had lit candles to pamper myself before the night out. It was comforting my body as I splashed the water over me, to remove the soap that covered parts of my body. I took a look at my hand and empty ring finger, and thought of how I wanted to be married as well.

However, Ra wasn't ready. I knew he had a lot of growing up to do. I sat and thought to myself, that I had everything that I could ask for, but I didn't have what I wanted the most. I wanted a family and a husband, but it wasn't the right timing.

I also thought about my future and my beliefs. Yes, I believe in God, but I felt like I needed to be more active with god. There have been times I just prayed asking god to lead me in the right direction. However, I felt that things were not going right. I figured it was because I wasn't living the lifestyle, he wanted me to live. I could remember my mother being very active with church and always putting God first. She was a Christian woman whose faith was dominant.

She had always told me to walk by faith and not my sight. My mother Beverly, would always stress to me about my faith, my religion, and that it is imperative to seek the Lord. Not because he is God, but because what he did for us. For the past three years, my faith has not been the same since she's been gone. My mom passed away to a terrible heart attack. I prayed, but it wasn't enough.

Last month I had a horrible miscarriage, that could have killed me. I stressed about finishing school and dealing with Ra's selfish ways. I lost my baby in the mix of it because of the stress. It took a while to let go, but sometimes I have my moments. I did not want any parts of myself, as well as Ra. I felt like I didn't love him as much once I lost the baby. It almost took a year to get myself back to where

I wanted to be, and also want to be a part of Ra's life. Maybe that's why he cheated on me, but it still wasn't an excuse for his selfish ways.

I knew I needed to have the Lord in my life. I had given up on myself and especially my faith. I needed the Lord to strengthen me, because I knew I was still dealing with issues that Ra did not understand. Losing my mother as well as my baby caused me to shut down. It was hard for me to pray. I felt that God was missing from me and I needed him back in my life.

After my long hot bath, I lotioned my body with "Beautiful Day" from Bath and Body Works, and the fragrance to go along. I then walked to my closet naked and pulled out my black panties set from Victoria Secret. I then pulled out my Balmain dress, that was a sequin mini dress that fit every curve of my body. The dress had a deep split in the front that exposed my cleavage and a little part of my stomach. I then picked out my sequin booties from Alexander Mc Queen, which had silver diamond studs that were displayed over my heels.

My hair was bone straight and fell 28 inches long. I made up my face with a Smokey eye shadow and nude lipstick. For some reason, the nude lipstick made my lips look a little plump, but not too much. I knew how to do makeup as well because I learned from YouTube videos. That was another hobby I sought. I then put on the 18k earrings that Ra had just gotten me, and the Rolex.

"Make love to me, when my days look low, pull me in close and don't let me go," was Ra's ringtone when he called. I walked over to the nightstand and unplugged my phone from the charger. "Hello…"

"Babe I'm downstairs," he said.

"Ok, I'm coming down now, "I said and hung up.

Perfect timing, I thought, and walked out of the room closing the door. I then went to the closet and took wee-wee pads out, and placed them on the floor for Diamond. Being that I didn't have any time to walk her, I figured I'd better set a few wee-wee pads on the floor. I poured her some food, and gave her a full bowl of fresh water in her dispenser. I heard her run out and watch me as I went to the closet.

I walked to the living room closet and pulled out my long, black, mink fur that hung to the ground. I put on my coat and grabbed the mask that sat on the shelf. The veil was clear with a rhinestone mask, that revealed my eyes. Taking the cover off the box, I placed it on my face. I had my phone and keys in my hand. I thought about a bag, but I decided not to bring one. I cut the light out and closed the door behind me. "See you later Diamond," I said, as I blew her a kiss.

As I walked outside the building, Ra was standing outside of his car on phone. He looked like he'd been waiting long. "Boy, what you are doing?" I asked looking at him.

When he heard my voice, he got off his phone and tucked it into his pants. Ra reached over and gave me a half hug with one arm behind his back. I sensed the smell of another women's fragrance was on his blazer. However, I didn't say anything. I was close, but ignored it and told myself I would let him know tomorrow, and let him know this had to stop.

I was not walking into the New Year with habits that took place in previous years. I knew a change had to be done. Breaking my thoughts, Ra then pulled his other hand from behind his back, revealing a white rose.

"Aww," I said, blushing but still pissed. I reached out to grab the rose anyway. He took my hand and walked me to the car. I was chuckling because he always knew how to set the mood. "Thank you, babe," I said, as he opened the car door. As I slid inside, he lifted up my coat so it wouldn't get caught in the door.

"You look beautiful as always," he said, getting inside the car. "Well thank you babe, you looking good yourself." Ra wore his black mink trench coat, with a Givenchy suit that was all black, and his Jimmy Choo loafers. He displayed his gold chain and the Rolex watch I got him. "I like your mask," he said, stopping at a red light. "Well thank you, where is yours?" I asked smirking. "In the back seat," he said and I smirked at him.

On the ride over the Manhattan Bridge, there was a little bit of a traffic jam. It was so packed that the line wasn't moving. However, being that it was a holiday, traffic was expected. "We're going to be late," I said. He laughed, "Girl, we always late, it's nothing new." "Well it's your birthday, you can be spoiled this one time," I said smirking.

"Girl where are yall at?" Kim asked in a text message. "We are in traffic," I typed, responding to her message. "Well yall need to hurry up," Kim typed. "In a few minutes," I typed responding back. "We are waiting on yall late asses," Kim typed. I laughed because Ra and I were always running late for every event. It was nothing new. Within a few seconds, I got a picture mail from Kim. "Wow!" I said. It was a picture of Kareem, Kim, Toast, and Tania. They took a couple's picture.

"Aww, you guys look nice, it's such a beautiful picture." I sent back via text. "Ra, look at them," I said showing him the picture. He glanced at the phone trying to keep his eyes on the road and he nodded because he was so focused on the road. "We knew we look good, now hurry yall late asses up," Kim sent via text message. I texted back to Kim an emoji of a fist and she texted back with three fists. I started laughing.

"Babe I can't wait for Kareem's proposal to Kim, I know she is going to be happy." For some reason, he ignored what I said and simply nodded to what I was saying. I could tell he was uncomfortable about talking about the proposal. Ra figured I was going to ask about marriage, but my pride wouldn't allow me to ask him. Ra and I had been together for about four years and marriage was forever.

CHAPTER 4

When we arrived, there were so many people waiting outside to get in. "Dang, babe," I said, as I watched the line of people. It looked like a party was going on outside as well. "Yeah, it is a lot of people," he said, backing up to a parking spot, that was right in front of Dumbo.

Ra helped me out of the car and held my hand as we walked towards the lounge. He always loved showing me off in front of people, and it made me feel special. Before we entered inside, the photographers snap pictures of Ra, and I; as we did our little pose.

"Wassup man?" Ra said to the bouncer, while giving him a dap. Cool was his name. "What up man, I see how you're moving," he said, as he unhooked the red velvet rope. Ra nodded his head as he walked through with me on his arm.

Cool was the bouncer and checked the guests in. There was a list of people I had to invite to come. If your name was not on that list, you were not allow to enter. I figured that's why it was so many people waiting outside.

As we walked through, Ra still had me on his arm. When we stepped inside there wasn't a large crowd, but there were more than enough people. I could breathe the fresh air. I spotted Tania and Kim where Ra and I were to be seated. Nearby, were Kareem and Toast taking shots.

"Hey!" I said, reaching my arms out giving Kim and Tania hugs and kisses. "Girl you look beautiful," Tania said, twirling me around. "Yass girl, Yass!" Kim said. I laughed at Kim's crazy self and said, "Thank you, ladies, yall look beautiful as well." "Happy Birthday bro!" Kim said hugging Ra. "Yass! Happy birthday old man!" Tania blurted out, as she chuckled. "Thank you, thank you," he said blushing.

"Wassup Tye? You look lovely as always", Kareem said, reaching out and hugging me. We all reached out giving each other hugs and showing mad love. It was always like that every time we linked up. We loved each other like sisters and brothers, and our circle stayed tight.

Toast was already tipsy. He always was turned up before the night ended. "Ty, Ty, hey girl," he said, holding two bottles in his hands, with his arms spread out. "Wassup Toast?" I said showing love back. "You hooked this party up," Kareem said, "Yes girl, it's beautiful in here, you did your thing," Kim said, taking a sip of her Patron.

"Thank You, thank you," I said proudly, and felt relieved because it was a success. "Just make sure you're available to plan my wedding," Kim said eyeing Kareem. I laughed and hit her on the shoulder, and thought to myself that Kim probably knows it's about to go down tonight. Kareem shook his head at Kim.

Kareem and Kim have been dating for 12 years now since they were teenagers and stayed together. I met Kim and Kareem through Ra. Once I became close to Kim, we've been good friends ever since. Kim's been throwing wedding bells at Kareem for a while and I guess it finally registered.

"Happy Birthday to my man RA!", the DJ shouted out, as 28 different sparkling drinks came our way. There were all kinds of liquor, such as Moet, which were two different kinds, Patron, 1800, Henny, and many more. So many bottles came towards our way with the DJ playing Go, Go, its ya birthday by 50 cents.

Ra was surprised and excited. I usually don't drink, but for one night it wouldn't kill me. Besides, it was my man's birthday celebration. I was going to celebrate with my man until I couldn't celebrate anymore. A night to new beginnings and life changes that would take place. I knew it would be a great way to bring in the New Year, with a birthday celebration. Maybe it would be an excellent way to see a different way of life. We were not getting younger, only older in time. Hopefully, good things happened to those who wait. Let's begin.

"You did a great job babe, I'm very proud of you" he said in my ear. I smirked, but I couldn't forget that fragrance. "It's all about you today, live for today," I said. He took a sip from his glass as he eyed me. I looked at him with a smile. He slapped me on the butt and poured me a cup of Moet, and that's when the celebration began.

The night was perfect and the crowd was live. We still managed to have space and breathing room. The food was gone, but the drinks were still being served. I was already tipsy, but I ignored the signs and still continued having a good time.

I had gone to the bathroom about ten times, with Kim having to help me. Once I relieved my bladder, I was back and ready to party. "The ball is about to drop!", the DJ said yelling out. "Ooh, babe, where you at?", I said looking around, noticing him behind me. He had a cup in his hand taking another shot. There were 30 seconds left until the New Year would begin.

"Before we let the ball drop, my man Kareem has a special announcement to make," the DJ announced. Kim was taking selfies, sitting next to Kareem. She didn't know the DJ was talking about her Kareem. Kareem stood up, and Kim tried getting up, but Kareem told her to sit back down. Kareem faced Kim as she looked up at him. She had a confused look on her face, but she wanted to know what Kareem was going to say.

The music stopped, and all eyes were aimed to Kareem and Kim. I started to smile because I had been waiting for this moment and now it was happening. For some reason, I felt like it was happening to me. Ra stood beside me, and I noticed from the corner of my eye, that he had seen my facial expression, but he turned his attention back to Kareem and Kim.

"Kim, I know I may not be the best person to get along with, and we've had our issues in the past. We've also dealt with some difficulties in the present, and you've given me a million chances." I wasn't sure what Kareem meant by current problems they had, but it didn't matter now. Everyone had issues in a relationship, I thought to myself. "I'm also bad with words or expressing myself in front of a room full of people, but you know my love for you is real. "Kareem said, expressing his love for Kim. I saw her eyes whelm up with tears. Of course, mine did the same. That's my girl, but I wasn't sure if it was the liquor or the excitement.

"You held me down, and I couldn't ask for anyone better. Forgive me if I can't bend on one knee, but I'm giving you my heart for a lifetime. Kimberly Mitch, will you be my wife?". So, without any words from Kim, she lifted up and kissed him on the lips. That was her way of saying I do. Kareem then slipped the ring on her finger and they shared another passionate kiss. The ring was beautiful. It was a band of Chanel-set, round brilliant diamonds. Which enhanced the classic Tiffany six-prong setting, for a spectacular display of white light.

"Aww," I said, putting my hands over my mouth. "Go, girl!" I yelled out. Ra did another peek from the corner of his eye and noticed my reaction towards Kim's new excitement. He took another sip of his drink and focused back on Kareem and Kim. The crowd went crazy. All kinds of yells, screams, and congratulations went out to Kareem and Kim. Of course, you had the haters saying negative things, but that didn't stop their joy.

"10 seconds left!" the DJ shouted out. "Ra that was a long ass 30 seconds" I whispered in his ears. "Yeah, right," he said. We both had a confused look on our faces. It felt like the night was slowing down. Everything was moving in slow motion. I couldn't tell if it was my imagination or the drinks, but everything was going slow "10...9...8...7..." as the crowd began the countdown for the New Year, and everybody was next to someone. The guys were with close friends or the ladies with their close friends and couples. Everyone was bringing in the New Year with someone who was special to them.

I held Ra's hand till the New Year began. I thought about the rough year I had last year. I wanted to put it in the past and start over with a new start. I felt it was going to be a good year. Who knows, maybe my Dream will come true with Ra and I'll have a family.

"6...5...4...3...2...1.... Happy New Year!" The crowd yelled out. As the Ball dropped, it exploded with glitter and black and silver party mixers. They busted out all over the crowd, while some popped bottles spraying them all over people. No one got mad, they all enjoyed it. It was beautiful! Everything around me was going in slow motion with excitement for the New Year.

I turned to look at Ra, and I kissed him on the lips. "Happy New Year's Baby!" "Same to you," he said kissing me with a slap on the butt. He then hugged me, and I hugged him back. Kim kissed her man while waving her ring and Tania kissed Toast, as he held his bottle in his hand. The night couldn't have been going any better.

"Let this be a Happy New Year, with many blessings and happiness," I said to Ra as I rocked and held him close to me. I left the past in the past and worried about the present and future. I completed my goal of finishing school and accomplished throwing one of the best parties of the New Year. I looked forward with new excitement for this year.

Who knows what this year will bring. I do know it will bring change and a new beginning. Let's see what 2013 will bring to me... Happy New Year! 2013

CHAPTER 5

Night and Day was beginning to merge in time. It was 4:30am and I was done. I couldn't count how many drinks I'd had, but running to the bathroom wasn't helping me at all. I couldn't stand nor barely walk anymore, I had no more strength. We all partied hard. Toast was still downing bottles. Tania had a headache and was ready to go. Kareem and Kim sat down still excited about their engagement. Ra and I sat watching everybody continue to celebrate the New Year. I was ready to go and couldn't wait to sleep the liquor off. It was so strange because I never drank, and for once I was completely wasted. I wasn't going to remember this night when I woke up. My head hurt like hell, and I could barely see anyone. However, I appeared sober because you couldn't tell I was drunk.

"Baby I'm ready to go," I said turning to Ra. My lips were perked up at him giving him a look. "Yeah me too," he said, taking another sip of his Patrón. "Aye, Reem!" Ra yelled out to Kareem, who was already walking towards our direction. However, Kareem already knew what time it was. Ra lifted me up, and we all gathered our things to end the night.

Kim was a little tipsy as Kareem held her. Ra held my hand to walk out, because if he wasn't by my side, I don't think I could have made it. Tania and Toast were arguing because, Toast was having too many drinks. "Don't tell me what to do:" he said, as he grabbed the bottle out of her hand. They were always arguing every time they were out, and Tania tried to stop him. Tania drunk a lot as well, but she knew her limit. I always thought she was turned out from drinking by Toast. Tania didn't know her level when it came to Toast. She would do anything to please him and made him her main priority.

Tania worshiped the ground Toast walked on, yet he did nothing but disrespect her. Rumor had it that he was very abusive when he drank, but Tania never told me about it. I never brought it up to her either. Tania and Toast were dating for six years. Tania and I were good friends, but we really never spoke heavy like Kim and I. Tania just was distance and it was just something about her I couldn't understand. But she was a cool person and fun to be around.

Toast and Ra were friends for a long time as well. They had met each other through Kareem and they was tight as well.

Kareem went to get Toast and Kim, and I went to talk to Tania. "You can't control him," Kim said. "You know how he gets, but you still manage to put yourself in an argument with him," Kim said. Kim always told Tania the truth and they would start arguing, but for some reason this time they didn't. "Yes, girl let him be," I said to her. "I know, I will," Tania said walking away from us. She walked behind Toast shaking her head, and I knew she was embarrassed again. I looked at Kim, and she looked at me. "Sometimes I wonder," Kim said, and I just shook my head. "I tell that girl all the time he needs help and if he won't get help to leave him. But nooo!" Kim said throwing her hands in the air. I agreed, but I knew everybody's relationship wasn't perfect, especially my relationship with Ra. Who am I to judge another person's relationship, but I do know to never let disrespect be acceptable.

Since I hired cleaners to clean up the party, I had to tell them to come back around noontime, because the party wasn't stopping any time soon. Thank God I was able to hold the place until the next day. The crowd got bigger and more people came. A fight already occurred, and Cool had to throw some people out. "Yeah, it's time to go now," Ra said.

One thing about Ra, he didn't like big crowds. He always felt like anywhere that had too big of a crowd he wouldn't be around or attend. We all walked towards the exit, and it was a struggle getting to the front, because a lot of people wouldn't move. I had to push my way through even though I didn't have the strength, but I still managed to get through. I couldn't wait to get out because I couldn't breathe. It was so dry and humid, that it was hard for me to catch my breath.

A hand grabbed mines, and when I turned to see who it was, I pulled it back. "Hey beautiful," a dark-skinned, handsome guy said. I ignored his comment and continued to push through the crowd. I then felt a hand grab my shoulder pulling me towards them. "My apology," the guy said, looking me in my face. "Don't touch me again," I said, and this time I pulled away pushing through the crowd.

I wondered where Ra was, but I didn't bother to turn around to see if he was behind me. I reached the front with Tania and Kim waiting by the door. "Girl we got to go, it's crazy in here," I said, as I walked up to them. "Where is Toast and them?" Tania asked. "I thought they were up here with yall," I said, turning back to see if they were behind us. "I guess we got to wait for them," Kim said, with her arms folded. I couldn't wait. I became so agitated, that my nerves started messing with me. The air made it hard for me to breathe and I didn't feel right. I was so upset about the guy grabbing up on me, that I needed to go right then.

Before I knew it, a fight broke out. Moreover, each of the parties began to argue. "They fighting!" Tania yelled out. "Oh, hell no we got to go! Ra! Ra!" I yelled out, as if he could hear me through all this noise. "I guess we have to meet them home," Kim said. "But I don't want to leave them," I said to Kim. Even though I didn't have any more energy, I suddenly had the urge to stay. "I will take you home, and you need to go home Tye because you're wasted," Kim said. She was right, but I still didn't feel right leaving him.

POP...POP...POPPPP... we all ducked covering our heads. "WTF!" I said. "Somebody is shooting!" somebody yelled out through the crowd.

I nearly jumped out of my skin and a little pee released from me. The sound of gunshots scared me. I looked to see where Kim was, and I saw her covering herself. I didn't see Tania. As we tried getting up to make it outside, the crowd bum-rushed us. I wound up losing my balance and falling to the ground, causing my phone to drop out of my hand and my coat as well.

All of a sudden, my eyes began to darken, and I was getting dizzy. So, I lay back on the ground trying to let the dizziness stop, but it started getting worst. My eyes widened, but it was turning dark. This time I tried lifting up, but I couldn't move. My legs were so weak that I couldn't feel my body. I felt paralyzed and heavy. I was so stiff that my body went into shock.

I tried to talk, but my mouth was numb. Everything from top to bottom wasn't moving, and I panicked slightly. I was numb, and my eyes were closing. I tried not to allow my eyes to close, but the darkness and dizziness I couldn't control. I squinted to see if Ra was near, but saw a moving crowd fading in and out. It was slow motion around me.

With one eye open and the other eye shut, it looked like a shadow was over me. "Babe" I softly said, because it was so hard for me to speak. Someone was reaching towards me, but I couldn't make out who it was. I couldn't see clearly, but it looked like a mask as the person got closer. My eyes were dark and dull, and at this time I couldn't see anything. Blackness was my vision, as I felt my body being lifted in the air. At that moment I completely blacked out...

CHAPTER 6

Ra...

Ra walked his way to the front exit. However, he didn't see Tye or the rest of his friends next to him. He turned around to see if they were behind him, but they weren't. Ra looked towards the section he thought he would see them, but they weren't there. He thought to himself, that they should be in the front waiting for him.

As Ra turned around to walk towards the front, he accidentally bumped into a guy who stood the same height as him. Before Ra could even apologize, the guy shouted at him. "Yo watch where the F you walking MAN!" The guy yelled in Ra's face.

Ra wanted to apologize, but the smart comment made him upset. Ra and the guy looked into each other's eyes, and Ra tried walking away. Ra knew if he didn't walk away, there was going to be a problem. As Ra proceeded to walk away, the guy grabbed Ra's arm towards him. "You heard what I said, watch where the F*** YOU WALK!" However, this time Ra spoke up, because that was the second time he tried getting slick. "Don't grab me!" Ra said, looking him dead in his face.

At this point, the guy got crazy. He was cursing, using foul language and spitting threats at Ra. So, Ra used the same type of style and tone to defend himself. The guy's group of friends came over surrounding Ra, putting Ra in the middle against them and him. "Nah you not going anywhere until you apologize to my man," one of his friends said, looking Ra in the face. Ra looked from the corner of his eye, still watching the guy he accidentally bumped.

"Damn," Ra said in his head, because he knew where this was going to lead. They were way too disrespectful, and Ra wasn't having anybody in his face disrespecting him. He thought the right thing to do was to walk away, but the drama still followed him.

"Man move out my way," Ra said, still making eye contact with the guy that stood in front of him. Cool was nowhere to be found, nor any of his friends, and Ra knew it was about to go down. Suddenly Kareem and Toast broke through the friends that had circled Ra in.

"F*** out my man's face!" Toast said, to the guy who stood on the side of Ra. This time Toast was all in the guy's face talking foul language to him, but it didn't make any difference. "Fame, that's my man, it's no problem," Kareem said, trying to peace up the drama between the two. Kareem stood in the middle between Fame and Ra. "Nah f*** that, ya man don't know how the f*** to walk and I'm not playing with him," Fame said with so much anger. You could tell Fame was very upset from the tone in his voice and the look in his eyes.

Fame was a well-known hustler who beat a body case a year ago. He was highly respected and had a name for himself in the streets. Fame was a cool person, but when he drank he was an entirely different person. Fame was the type of person you didn't want to have an issue with. He was well known for dropping bodies.

Ra, on the other hand, wasn't a street person, but he also wasn't a punk. Ra had another side of him as well, but never wanted anybody to see that side of him. If you took it there though, it was a side of Ra you didn't want to see. Ra did have a name for himself, but he knew how to carry himself. "Kareem, I don't have time for this," Ra said seriously looking at Kareem. Kareem knew his friend didn't want any problems. "Let's go, Kareem!", Ra said walking away. Fame reached over Kareem and punched Ra on the side of his face. Fame hit Ra so hard that he busted the side of Ra's lip.

Ra almost lost his balance, then charged back, punching Fame in the face. Fame fell to the floor, dropping something out of his hand. Ra touched the side of his face, and it was already swollen with blood gushing out. He looked at his hand and then at Fame, then noticed he was hit with the butt of a gun. Ra became very upset and saw nothing but black.

Fame got up rushing Ra, knocking him into the DJ stand. Ra was leaning against the DJ almost falling, but got the strength to push Fame against the wall. Fame and Ra were fighting, and there was nothing anybody could do to break them up.

After the first punch was thrown at Ra, Fame's group of friends started fighting Kareem. Most of Kareem and Ra's friends jumped into the fight as well, and both parties were fighting one another.

No one could have stopped what was going on. Others stayed to watch the fight, but most left because gunshots were let off in the air. Bottles, tables, chairs and everything were being thrown around. It was starting to become chaotic.

As Ra and Fame continued to fight, it started to become a death match. Fame tried grabbing the gun he hit Ra with, wanting to shoot him, but Ra grabbed Fame's hand aiming it towards the ceiling. Fame blasted more shots with Ra holding his hand. There was a tug of war between the two trying not to get shot.

Within a couple of minutes, police came rushing through, breaking up the brawl. They had arrested each group of people that were a part of the fight. Most of them got away, but others were arrested. Fame and Ra were still going at it aggressively towards one another.

The police spotted Ra on Fame giving him several blows to the face. They rushed over and grabbed Ra off of Fame.

They then slammed Ra to the ground trying to control him. Ra was not aware of what was happening, so he reacted differently. Ra was in a rage and still in black out mode. Ra tried fighting off whoever was on him, before noticing it was the police. He then calmed down and held his composure.

Several police officers came rushing over trying to put Ra down. One policeman held Ra's head, pressing it down on the wet floor. Another policeman held his knee in Ra's back was, while the other policeman put the handcuffs on his wrist. The policeman that had his knee in Ra's back reading him his rights. Ra laid there with three police officers on him and noticed that Fame wasn't moving. Fame was slouched over on his side. Ra watched what the policemen were doing, and saw they were checking his pulse. They checked his neck and wrist and still there was no movement from Fame.

Within moments the paramedics came rushing over to Fame's slumped body. They checked for a pulse too, and there was no movement. Ra tried lifting his head a little, but the policeman put more pressure on it. "Don't move!", the policeman yelled out and dug his knee harder in Ra's back. However, Ra couldn't help the squirming because he was shocked that Fame wasn't moving.

Damn, I know he's not dead, he could just be knocked out, Ra thought in his head. Ra became a little nervous about the whole thing, and he couldn't control his movement. Ra noticed the paramedics lift Fame's body onto the stretcher and saw puddles of blood drip as they lifted him up. Ra freaked out causing more movement, not realizing the policemen were still on him. Ra wasn't paying any attention to what was happening around him and suddenly felt a stinging sensation in his eyes.

The policeman sprayed mace directly in his eyes causing Ra to lift up. With three policemen on him, Ra managed to knock them off of him while moving frantically because of his eyes. He tried covering his eyes by squinting, and the policeman sprayed more mace. This time Ra screamed out, "My eyes, my fucking eyes!As he yelled out, he wallowed all over the floor, squinting his eyes.

They took their sticks out and started beating Ra. They hit and poked him as he moved on the floor, but he couldn't control his movement because his eyes were on fire. Ra yelled out as his eyes burned some more. This time the three policemen picked Ra up and slammed him to the floor. They dragged and pulled him on the wet sticky floor, and then outside to the slippery and damp concrete.

It was starting to snow with thick snowflakes that left puddles of snow and water. As they pulled Ra into the cold air, they threw him again on the wet concrete floor. However, this time he felt his mouth lump up some more. The police picked him up to his own two feet, but Ra could barely walk because his eyes was still burning. They escorted him to a nearby van, where other people were arrested.

"My eyes, my eyes, give me something for my eyes!", Ra said with mucus and blood running down his mouth. However, the police ignore him and continue to pull him into the van. Being that it was hard for him to see, he stumbled trying to sit.

At this time the crowd that was inside, was now outside watching what the police were doing. People whispered amongst one another, knowing Ra didn't deserve that treatment. "Let him go!" someone yelled out in the crowd.

Ra tried squinting one eye open, leaving the other eye closed, but it still burned him. He saw a little light, but it was blurry. He saw shadows of people around him and closed his eyes again. Ra could tell his eyes were beginning to swell because of the numbness around them. He rocked back and forth trying to control the burning from his eyes, but it didn't help. Tears leaked out of his eyes from the mace that had been sprayed twice. It was still hard for Ra to sit down.

As he felt the movement from the van in motion, he didn't imagine his night would end like this. With everything black and blurry, he realized his New Year would be the beginning of a senseless year.

CHAPTER 7

Ra...

As Ra tried opening his eyes, they were still painful with a burning sensation. His eyes inflated from the mase and the fight from the other night. Ra eyes were closed shut, and he could barely move. His strength was weak, especially his back. Bruises were all over his arms, with knots on his knees. Ra didn't understand his surroundings and couldn't remember what happened. He was completely confused about how he wound up in jail and couldn't wait to speak to a guard.

As he looked around his cell, he couldn't believe it. He looked across from his cell and noticed a guy across. Ra tried lifting up to see if he saw a guard, but his strength wouldn't allow him. Everything hurt him. Ra thought for a minute that he was jumped or robbed, because he could not remember anything.

Ra had little strength to pull himself up. As he lifted up, he slightly yelled from the pressure in his back and realized his leg were in pain. He limped toward the bars of the cell to look for a guard. Ra didn't see any guards within sight and didn't know what to do at this point. He didn't have access to a phone or anything.

Wondering how he got himself into this drama, he limped back to his dirty bed and sat on the edge of it. He then placed his hands covering his head, trying to remember what happened, but nothing came to mind. Ra felt a stinging sensation on his lip, and noticed a huge knot. He then examined his face with his hands and felt several scratches and bruises on his face.

Ra sat there thinking of different scenarios as to what could have happened, as guard came yelling his name. Ra recognized the familiar voice and immediately looked up. To Ra's surprise, it was a good friend of his from the past. "Reggie?" he asked, looking out the cell and limping his way towards the bars. "Ra, Ra!" he said, surprised to see him. "Yo Ra, I wasn't sure if it was you, but the name had me thinking it was."

Reggie was a good friend of Ra. They grew up together in New Brunswick, NJ. Their parents were best friends, and they were more like brothers. When Ra's mother died, Reggie's mother took custody of Ra. Reggie and Ra attended Howard University together. After college, Reggie moved to Atlanta to produce music, and Ra moved to New York to finish his Masters. They lost contact after college but remained friends and were more like brothers.

"Reggie, what's going on?" Ra asked. He was feeling a little relieved. He noticed Reggie staring at his face and could tell he was in bad shape. Reggie pretended that he didn't see his friend's bruises.

"Reggie please tell me what's going on?" "Why am I in here?" Ra asked with a concerned look on his face. Ra saw the expression on Reggie's face and knew there wouldn't be any good news. "Ra what happened last night?" Reggie asked. "It was my birthday, and I celebrated at Dumbo Lounge with a few friends," Ra said, telling Reggie the story, not knowing why he was in there.

Reggie looked at his friend and stared at him like he was crazy. "Ra, don't tell me you don't remember what happened last night," Reggie said, shaking his head. Ra didn't remember what happened last night. All he could remember was celebrating his birthday with his friends. However, Ra didn't want to tell Reggie he didn't remember what took place. Reggie knew that Ra didn't remember what happened yesterday, because of the expression Ra gave him.

'Ra, you don't remember, do you?" Reggie said, leaning against the cell. Ra nodded his head no with his back against the cell. "Ra look at me," Reggie said. Ra slowly turned around careful not to hit any of the bruises that were on his body.

"Ra I'm not supposed to tell you this, but you know I have to let you know what happened. They said you murdered someone". Ra gave Reggie a look like he was crazy and couldn't believe what he'd just heard.

Ra stared in a state of stock, making it hard for him to speak. "What!" Ra said, with a weird facial expression. "Reg, I didn't kill nobody, what are you talking about?" he asked, only this time raising his voice a little. "Ra lower your voice…" Reggie said. "Look, Reggie, what do you mean murder? I didn't kill anybody" Ra said, with anger in his voice. "Ra I'm just telling you what I heard," Reggie said expressing himself. "You were all over the news, media and every-where, but I wasn't sure if it was you or not".

"Damn Reggie this has to be a dream," Ra said. "Yeah man, they said he was shot in the stomach and chest and was bleeding internal-ly. Also, they stated a girl was shot too and paralyzed". "What?" Ra asked, because he couldn't believe what he just heard. He didn't want to hear anything that Reggie had to say because he felt sick. Ra was in denial about what he was being told.

Everything around Ra was going in slow motion. "Damn, what have I gotten myself into?" Ra said, as all these thoughts came run-ning into his head. Ra shook his head in disbelief. "Ra you heard me, man?" Ra snapped out of his daze and nodded his head to Reggie.

"Do you now remember what happened that night?" Reggie asked Ra. He still didn't have a clue as to what happened that night though. "I seriously can't remember what happened that night Reggie, between you and me," Ra said.

"Do you remember giving your statement to the police?" Reggie asked. Ra was just deaf to the questions Reggie asked him. Ra did forget the statement he made to the police. Everything was a blank, and he couldn't remember anything.

"Ra, you have to remember what happened, because when you go to court, they are going to use your statement," Reggie said. "I know Reggie, but nothing is coming to mind. I can't remember what took place at all. All I can remember is walking out of the lounge with my girl". Reggie shook his head, "Well Ra, think about it. Maybe you will remember soon. I have a good lawyer you can use as well, he beats murder cases like it's nothing" Reggie said. Ra wasn't even thinking about that. He was still trying to fathom murdering someone.

"Ok Reggie, thanks man," Ra said silently. There was just too much information to remember. I woke up in a cell to a murder case, Ra thought to himself. "Calm down and gather your thoughts," Reggie said. He felt bad for his friend, because he knew he wasn't in good shape.

"I will try," Ra said in a low tone. "You have a visit today, so they will come to pick you up in a little while." However, Ra wasn't up to seeing anyone in his condition or looking like he did. He figured he'd stay in his cell and think, but he probably needed to see somebody besides these grey walls. Reggie reached between the bars and gave Ra a pound. "You will be ok Ra," Reggie said looking at Ra and walked off.

Ra slowly made it back to his bed and put his head down. He had a nervous feeling in his stomach. The words murder made him sick, and the worst part was that he couldn't even remember what took place. "Damn I've been in the worst situations and never thought I'd ever be behind bars. Ra rocked his body back and forth trying to control his nerves, and the butterflies going through his stomach.

Ra got up pacing back in forth, trying to calm his nerves. He felt like he had to use the bathroom. His nerves had his stomach doing flips, but he ignored it. Ra thought about the girl who was shot. He couldn't believe he had to deal with the weight of that on his mind as well. Everything went through his head about his life and what would happen next. Ra heard keys and knew it was a guard coming. "You have a visitor," the short, brown skinned, female guard said, standing by the cell.

She opened the up the gate and escorted him from his cell to visit. Ra didn't know who was visiting him, but he never cared to ask who it was. He didn't want to see Tye looking the way he did, but it did not matter at this point. Ra's mind drifted off to another place.

CHAPTER 8

It was 12:30 pm when Ra went downstairs into a holding cell, to wait for his visit. It was perfect that his visitor came, because he didn't want to sit worrying about the possibility of conviction. Ra did all the procedures before visitation by getting search. Ra had to go through all the procedures of being searched before his visit. He was ordered to pull his jumper down, squat, then bend over and cough. Once he was finished getting searched, he was able to meet with his visitor.

Walking through the doors, he looked around the room and noticed two CO's on the visitation floor. One pointed him in the direction of where his visitor sat. It was Kareem sitting near the far-left side. Ra nodded his head as he walked toward Kareem. "Wassup?" he said, giving Kareem a pound. Kareem got up to greet him. "Wassup?" Kareem said looking at Ra. He noticed the bruises that were on Ra and tried not to stare at them. "Damn, they did some damage to you," Kareem said. "Hell yeah, I noticed my face as I was coming down," Ra said touching his bruised mouth.

"Kareem, what happened that night?" Ra asked jumping straight to the point. Kareem didn't remember that night either. He just stated what he heard from the news. "To tell you the truth, I don't remember much of that night either Ra. All I remember is us all walking out together" Kareem said. "Man, they said I murdered someone. Who did I murder? Did you know him?" Ra asked.

"Yeah, this dude named Fame. Kareem said. "I used to do some work with him a minute ago. He was a cool guy and well respected. It bugs me out because according to the newspaper, it all started over a bump to the shoulder. I know he couldn't have gotten that mad over that though." Kareem said. "I know it had to be something personal for Fame to react like that". Ra looked down and still couldn't believe it.

"Were you strapped that night?" Kareem asked Ra. "No, why would I need my gun". Ra carried a registered gun, but it was for his business needs. "I didn't have anything on me that night," Ra said. "Then I don't know how they are saying you killed him because they found a gun, and it wasn't even on you," Kareem said telling Ra. "Yeah this is bugged out to me Kareem. I don't even remember what happened to me, and all I'm hearing is hearsay," Ra said. Ra was still in stock.

"I know what you mean because I don't know what happened either," Kareem said, putting his head down. "The sad part Kareem is, I'm not sure if I did it or not. I know before I take this to court, I have to remember something." Ra said telling Kareem. "Did you speak to Tye? How is she doing?" Ra asked with a concerned look on his face, but Kareem didn't want to say anything. "I haven't heard from her," Kareem said. "I know she's been calling you Kareem, its ok, tell me," Ra said shaking his head.

Kareem sat quietly, but he knew he had to tell Ra what happened to Tye. "Ra, shit crazy man" Kareem said with his arms crossed. "What you mean?" Ra asked, with a confused look on his face. "Tye got shot and she's paralyzed." Ra looked at Kareem as if he was telling a lie. Ra shook his head breathing deeply. Then it suddenly hit him that's the girl that Reggie had told him about, but didn't know it was Tye.

A tear slid down his face, causing his bruise to sting. "You good man?" Kareem asked looking at Ra. Ra just stared in a daze of silence. "Did you see her?" Ra asked softly. "No, but Kim has been at the hospital every day. Kim told me Tye is in a coma. It's not looking good Ra, I'm sorry to say, "Kareem said. He didn't want to tell Ra about Tye's condition, because he knew he had to deal with the murder over his head.

Ra began to get angry with himself and wondered how this could have happened. "Kareem all I can remember about that night is, we all were walking out. This is some bullshit that is happening" Ra said. "It can't be real Kareem, I must be in a dream," Ra said. At this point he was beyond stressed. It felt crazy hearing what he had to hear right then. He sat in silence with a blank expression.

"Mills, Hector......!" the Guard yelled out. The visit was ending, as the guard yelled out more names. Without anything being said, Ra got up and Kareem did too, slightly hugging one another. "You'll be home soon," Kareem whispered in Ra's ear." Ra couldn't say anything back because, he was so messed up in his mind, that he felt lost. Ra just nodded his head and walked to where the guard stood.

"Call me later, I already put money in your account!" Kareem yelled out. Ra dragged his leg as he exited out of the visiting room. Ra didn't bother to look back as he continued to walk towards the guard. Kareem just sat there waiting to be called to leave the visiting floor. He wondered about his friend and didn't know what to do, except pray for him. Kareem thought deep inside that Ra was innocent. He wasn't the type to hurt anyone.

Ra lined up to go back to his depressing cell, with a lot on his mind. He worried about Tye and how he wished he could be there by her side. He needed to talk to her and see her. How could this have happened? I swore I was next to her, he thought to himself. Ra would have never put Tye in a compromising position if he knew he was in trouble, or if trouble was around them.

Ra was in the daze, and his surroundings moved slowly. He heard a voice say "Yo," from the side of him and turned to see who it was. A punch hit him directly in his face, almost knocking him down. With nothing said, Ra turned back around knocking the assailant straight on the ground. He looked to see who it was and didn't recognize him. Suddenly the guard pushed him back to the wall, telling him not to move. Ra held his hand up as blood dripped from his mouth. Ra's cut had reopened once the punch hit him.

She looked at him and noticed he was calm, but she still called for backup. Several officers ran down, while Ra stood against the wall holding his hands up. The guard rushed over grabbing the other man who was trying to get at Ra, and held him down. "You killed my brother and you are going to die," the guy said, while on the ground. The guard held the guy up moving him away from Ra.

As he tugged and pulled yelling threats, the guard proceeded to take him down the hall. "Are you ok?" she asked, looking at Ra. It was the same short, brown skinned guard that took him down for his visit. Ra nodded his head, wiping the blood from his mouth. She knew he didn't start the fight and told him to get back on line.

You have to go to the nurse so she can take care of your mouth. Ra said ok, limping back onto the line and proceeded back to his cell. He didn't know why she didn't put him in the hole, but he felt relieved. Thank you, God, he whispered to himself.

CHAPTER 9

Tye

BEEP...BEEP...BEEP...BEEP... was the sound of an irritating noise ringing in my ears, while my eyes were closed. The beeping noise began to get louder and annoying. I slowly opened my eyes to a bright light that beamed in my face. My eyes burned from the brightness of the hospital room. I circled my eyes around to adjust the blurriness, as I opened my eyes. I kept blinking to restore my vision clearly.

After a couple of times blinking, my eyes came into focus. As I tried lifting up slowly, my strength wouldn't allow me. I was weak in my arms and lower back. I then realized my surroundings, and became confused. Am I in the hospital? I questioned myself as I gathered my strength. "Ahhh..." I winced as I lifted up. I laid back down because the pain was unbearable. I moved my head around to see if anyone was there, and saw no one in sight.

My entire body was sore, and I could feel the cuts and bruises that were on my body. My legs, arms, and back were sore. I was a little swollen in those areas too. I then realized my lower end was patched up. I wondered what happened, and figured I must have been in a car accident leaving the party. I reached for the hospital phone and dialed Ra's phone, but it went straight to voicemail. I then called my phone, and it went straight to voicemail as well.

I finally had the strength to pull myself up, slouching trying not to sit up straight. However, that made the pain worse. I yelled in pain again, and suddenly the nurse came running in. "Miss, please lay back down, you need to rest." the middle aged, Spanish lady said holding my back, helping me lay back down. I did as she said and eased down slowly. Within a few minutes, Kim and Tania came walking in.

"You're up!" Tania said, walking towards my left side. Kim came to where the nurse was helping me back down and didn't realize she almost knocked the nurse down. "Excuse me!" the nurse said looking at Kim, but Kim ignored her, keeping her focus on me. The nurse then brushed past Kim, rolling her eyes and mumbled something in Spanish. She then stormed out closing the door.

"Tye are you ok?" Kim asked, reaching down to hug me. "I'm sore as hell, my body aches and I feel weak," I said. "What happened last night?" I asked, holding my hand over my head. Tania and Kim looked at one another giving a disappointed and bitter look. "Were we in a car accident? It feels like something beat me up," I said. As I spoke about how much pain I was in, they sat quietly, looking down at me. "What's wrong?" I asked the both of them, and they stayed silent. Kim rubbed my forehead gently, while Tania grabbed my hand. I already knew it was going to be bad news, but I was hoping it wasn't.

"Oh, can someone call Ra, because his phone is going straight to voicemail? Where is my phone? I need my phone. They stood there as if I weren't even talking. "Tye!" Kim said holding her composure. "It's January 5th," she said, as I had on a confused look. I thought to myself and I knew yesterday was Ra's birthday and wasn't sure if she knew the days.

"Huh! Kim, I'm lost", I said, with a confused look on my face. "Tye! you were in a coma for a couple of days." Tania held my hand while Kim grieved about my coma. "A coma?" I asked so confused. "What do you mean a coma?" I asked trying to lift up, but Kim told me to stay down. "What happened? Where is Ra? Is he ok?" I was asking so many questions because I became utterly lost about everything.

"Tye, after the party there was a fight and gunshots went off. People ran your way and knocked you down. Do you remember anything?" Kim asked, trying to refresh my memory. The only thing I could remember was leaving out of the lounge with Ra. "Kim, Ra and I left the lounge together and got inside the car, because we parked in front of Dumbo. That's the only thing I can remember Kim."

"No Tye, Ra was in back of us, and we had to wait in the front." I didn't remember what Kim was talking about, because I swore, I was in the car. The last thing I remembered was being with Ra. I thought Kim had lost her mind because she wasn't making any sense, and I was beginning to get very confused. "Ok, where is Ra?" I asked looking at Tania and Kim. "At least somebody could tell me what is going on here."

"I feel like somebody is hiding something from me and doesn't want to tell me. You guys know I am not too fond of secrets, so stop holding back", I said with a little attitude. "Tye you got shot in the back," Tania said. "Shot!" I said, with my hands over my mouth. "Yes, Tye you were shot by a stray bullet and was almost paralyzed," Kim said. Tears welled up in my eyes causing me to shake a little.

"Where is Ra then?" I asked, with tears pouring down my face. The tears burned the cuts that were on the side of my face. My nerves were acting up, and I couldn't control the shaking that overcame my body. "Someone call Ra," I said softly. I dried the tears that dripped down my face with my bruised-up hand.

Tania held her head down wiping the tears from her face. Kim sat on the bed holding my hand. She then leaned over and said "I

LOVE YOU" to me. "I could have lost you to that bullet" Kim expressed. I couldn't help but cry, and I kept crying, because I was still in shock from what they had just told me. It felt like I was going crazy because that's not what I remembered. I thought to myself but couldn't remember what happened that night.

Tania wiped the tears that fell from my face, and rubbed my hair back from my face. "Tye you were in a coma for five days and we've been up here every day," Kim said. "Thank you, I love yall," I said softly, because I was too choked up to talk.

At this point I was so hurt and vulnerable, that I felt a little better having them by my side. However, I also knew I needed to speak to Ra. For some reason, I felt something terrible had happened to Ra. "Where is Ra?" I asked dryly, making eye contact with Kim and Tania. I'd asked several times about Ra, and neither one of them would tell me anything. I felt like they were trying to avoid my question, so I knew it had to be something bad.

Tania got up to use the bathroom, excusing herself from the question. I turned my attention to Kim. "Tye, Ra is locked up." I suddenly began to panic. "Locked up? What do you mean Kim?" Kim looked me dead in the face and said, for murder. "Ra murdered someone that night in the club" she said. At that point everything was moving in slow motion. The words murder frightened me to tears. It ticked my nerves, because never in a million years could I imagine Ra murdering someone.

"Not Ra? Ra is no murderer" I said to Kim, with look of uncertainty. "Kim are you sure?" I asked, hoping she was wrong. Kim just nodded her head, turning it away from me. My throat closed in, and I suddenly began to get a rush. I ignored the signs. Tears dripped down Kim's face, leaking onto the hospital sheets. I laid there in silence, and I couldn't control the rush that was going through my body. I began to breathe deep, which caused my chest to sink in. It was hard for me to inhale as if I were having a heart attack.

Tania came out of the bathroom and noticed that I was gasping for air. "Tye! Calm down!" she said rushing to my side. Kim lifted up her head and noticed how I was reacting. "Calm down Tye, calm down," As they both tried to calm me down, the nurse came rushing in. "What's happened to her?" the nurse asked looking at Kim. Kim was in shock and couldn't get the words out. "Please, you ladies must leave immediately," the nurse said. Tania and Kim didn't want to leave me like that, so it was hard for them to follow her orders.

As the nurse pushed them out, the doctors came rushing in. They closed the door behind Tania and Kim and started working on me. "I don't want to leave her," Kim said with tears coming down. Tania said, "Me either", as they both walked down the hall waiting for me to get out of recovery.

Within a few hours, the doctors went out to talk to Kim and Tania, and informed them I was ok. "She was under a lot of stress that caused her body to react in a hypo tensive manner, but she is ok. "You ladies are welcome to see her". "Thank you, Doctor," Kim said, as she dried the teardrops from her face.

As they entered the room, I was lying in bed in silence. I didn't bother to lift up or anything. I just stared at the ceiling as Kim and Tania spoke to me. Words wouldn't leave my mouth, so I just listened to what Kim and Tania were saying. I was in a complete blurr and couldn't understand how this happened.

As I heard my friends speaking, I just said a silent prayer to God. "Lord I know it may seem as bad as it looks, but I also know that you are a higher power and the Almighty God. You have the last say so in all of this. Lord, please lead us in the direction you want us to follow, a path that will glorify you. I am asking for your help more than anything, and Lord you will help us along the way. In JESUS NAME AMEN! "I yelled out. "AMEN, AMEN" I repeated to myself over and over, with my hands raised in the air. Kim and Tania just held each other, as I called on the Lord's name.

CHAPTER 10

I entered my home to a strong odor. It was dark, cold and extremely smelly. As I cut on the light, I noticed the black poop and dried up pee stains that were on my rug. Wee-Wee pads were ripped up and scattered throughout the house. As I closed the door, I heard little footsteps coming my way. "Diamond!" I said, as she entered with tissue on her paw. I slowly bent down and picked her up.

She was so excited to see me. She couldn't control her excitement. Diamond wiggled, licked and wagged her tail as I petted her all over. "Were you being a good girl?" I asked, as I walked over to the couch placing my bag on it. Entering the kitchen, I saw a big mess. Her dog food was coming out of the ripped bag. I could tell she bit through the bag of food, by the way it was torn at the bottom.

Diamond was smart, and I couldn't be mad at her. I did leave her alone in the house for three weeks. Diamond's dispenser was half empty. I placed her down, and she looked up at me. I grabbed a bottle of water, and poured some in her dispenser. I spoiled Diamond. She didn't drink tap water, only FIJI bottled water. I then cleaned the dog food that was spilling out of the bag and poured her some more food.

Diamond devoured her food. As she ate, I watched her wag her tail. I walked out of the kitchen slowly, then bent down to pick up the dirty rug. The rug was full of stains and poop. I grabbed a big garbage bag under the kitchen sink, and put the dirty rug in it. I then grabbed the mop and pail and poured some hot water and bleach into the bucket. I couldn't mop the floor hard like I wanted to, because my back was still in pain. So, I quickly cleaned over the entire living room floor into the kitchen.

My house smelled much better now. I plugged in my Air Wick, and the smell began to permeate. I then lit a candle to enhance the scent even more. As I walked towards the room, it smelled like something was spoiled. It was coming from my bedroom. I opened the door with my light blinking on and off. I went out to the linen closet and switched the light bulb. I left my lights on all this time, I thought to myself. The sour smell was Ra's birthday cake I had made for him. It was hard as a rock and molded all around. Little gnats flew over the spoiled cake, and that too needed to be thrown away now.

I pulled the garbage that I had in the living room to the back and tossed the cake into the bag. I put my pretty red ribbon on my headboard, and picked up the remaining pieces of paper, that were on the floor. I then took off my sheets that needed to be changed. As I dumped the pillow out of the pillowcase, the card that Ra gave me fell out.

I sat on the bed and opened the card to read it. It slightly smelled like Ra's scent, and I remembered Ra leaving a card the night of his birthday.

"*Tye,*

You are worth more than diamonds and roses. I could never replace such a phenomenal woman. I am so proud of you and what you've been able to accomplished. I can't think of anyone I'd rather bring in the New Year with. I promise this year will be better than your last. I just hope it's not too late. See you tonight.

Love always

Ra"

I re-read the card over and over again, as if he'd just handed me the card. Tears welled up in my eyes, causing me to gasp for air.

Damn you Ra! I said to myself, as the card dropped out of my hand. You were right next to me, and we were almost home. I shook my head thinking to myself, as the tears still came down. My hurt and pain caused me to gasp.

Diamond looked to see me crying and came over to cheer me up, but I didn't pay her any attention. She then jumped up on my bed and rubbed her body against me. That was her way of comforting me. I picked her up and held her, as tears ran down my face. My mind blanked out, and crazy thoughts were in my head about that night. I just wished I could remember what happened, but my memory still hadn't come back. The sound of my house phone broke my silence. I slowly snapped back into reality and picked up the phone.

"Hello?" I said dryly…

"You have a collect call from?" "Rasheem" Ra's voice spoke. "An inmate at Rikers Island…" suddenly my silence broke, and for some reason I became nervous. I dried my tears with my t-shirt and moved Diamond to the side. I then pressed 1… "Hello…Hello…" Ra said.

"Ra Hello," I said. I couldn't have been more happy to hear his voice.

"Tye, your home, are you ok?" he asked.

I could barely hear him. Ra's voice was low over the phone. "Hello, baby I can't hear you," I said, getting off the bed to walk near the window "You hear me now?" he asked sounding low. I still couldn't hear him, so I smashed the phone to my ear, pressing hard so I could listen to him. However, it was so low and staticky I couldn't hear much.

"Are you ok?" I asked him. He ignored my question, and asked me if I could visit him tomorrow. "Yeah, I can come tomorrow." "Good," he said. Ra was saying something else, but I couldn't hear him. "Ra repeat that, I can't hear you." Without another word the phone clicked. "Hello…hello…" the dial tone came on.

I became so mad that I couldn't even cry. It had been three weeks and the first call I got, the phone hung up. Oh no, Ra must come home. Do I have to deal with this for the rest of my life? All these thoughts ran through my head as I tried calming down. I couldn't stress too much, because I still wasn't completely healed. The pressure wasn't healthy. "I know you are here Lord", I said to myself.

I wondered was this going to be our life forever. Was the interrupted phone calls and low pitch tone forever? Walking into the bathroom, I needed to take a hot shower to calm my nerves. I ran myself a shower to ease my mind and back pain. I hadn't showered in so long, because I was in the hospital. I knew I needed a shower badly. I slowly took off my clothes and couldn't help but notice the patched-up wound on my lower back.

I began to cry, realizing how life is too short. I could have been paralyzed or dead. All I could do was thank God. What could have been the worst tragedy in life, managed to be another chance. *"God you spared my life, you protected me from harm's way and guided me to another day. You didn't just save my life, but Ra lives as well, because he could have been gone as well. Even though I don't know what took place that night, if he is guilty, I pray that I'm strong enough to deal with it. God, I know he is a good man, and deep down I believe he is innocent. But it's you that has to determine that. I ask forgiveness for Ra and myself Lord. I pray for strength, health, my mind, and soul. I may not know the answer to what might happen at this point, but I do pray we get out of this situation. We are not perfect Lord, but we do mean well. If I've forgot or haven't told you this Lord, I want to thank you for everything you've done for me. Amen!"*

I looked into the mirror with a smirk and thought things may be tough as of now, but we would make it. I pulled the shower curtain back and eased my way into the steamy hot water...

As the shower rained on my body, my muscles began to relax. I was feeling better and more tranquil. I couldn't stop thinking how Ra was not here with me. Sleeping alone every night just gave me the creeps. I knew this could not be the end. I needed to visit Ra tomorrow. My doctors told me I needed to get rest, but I needed to see Ra.

Since I had to go all the way to Queens, I knew it would be a journey. I just had to be there for him. As I finished my shower, I dried off and put on a t-shirt. I then laid down to prepare for tomorrow. I felt comfortable as if Ra was next to me, but it was only Diamond. For the moment, I was pleased. Before I knew it, I was sound asleep.

CHAPTER 11

The next morning, I got up at 6 am. I was not sure what time visitations started, but I knew I had to be there early. I had already showered last night, so I just washed-up and brushed my teeth. I walked Diamond really quick and came back upstairs to get dressed.

I wore my gray, True Religion sweat suit and black construction Timbs. I did not have time to straighten my hair, so I did a quick wash, letting my natural curls flow. Ra loved when I wore my natural curls. He always thought they brought out a wild side of me. The least I could do, was make him feel good. Before leaving the house, I made sure to grab the dirty rug and garbage to be thrown out. I also made sure Diamond had fresh water and food.

Walking down the hall, I saw Mrs. Reed leaving the dumpster room. Mrs. Reed was my neighbor who lived on the same floor as Ra and me. I usually held short conversations with her from time to time, especially during the holidays. I wasn't in the mood to answer any questions about Ra, and I knew she would ask me something.

"Good Morning Hun…" Mrs. Reed said, as she held the door open for me to enter the dumpster. "Good Morning Mrs. Reed," I said rolling my eyes, hoping she didn't ask me about Ra. I threw the trash down the dumpster, and Mrs. Reed waited until I walked out. "Thank you for holding the door," I said, walking out of the dumpster room. I walked past, and I could feel her staring at me from behind.

I pressed for the elevator, and Mrs. Reed was still behind me. "You know I'm not the type to be in anybody's business, but I must say that Mr. Mills is a bad man." It was so hard for me to ignore her comment, so I had to give it to her. "Bad man? What do you mean by that?" I asked with my arms folded and left eyebrow arched. She looked at me as if she was disgusted and blurted out "Murder! He is a Murderer!"

"Murderer!" I said as I stared at her. I couldn't believe she'd just called Ra a murderer. My first thought was to beat the shit out of her. But I knew if I did that, I would be locked up for murder too. So, I kept my cool, but I had to tell Mrs. Reed about herself. "Murderer? Who did Rasheem murder?" I asked with a nasty attitude. She just looked at me confused, like she couldn't believe the words that left my mouth.

"Before you say anything that pertains to my man, get your facts straight. You have no idea what you're talking about, so I think its best you shut up. Now I happen to respect you, but don't let my respect turn into disrespect." I said smiling. "Have a Blessed day!" The elevator came at perfect timing, and I walked inside it, with other people on it. I turned and saw her with her mouth wide open in such disbelief, as she stared at the elevator door closing.

As I rode down in the elevator, I couldn't wait to leave. I was so, pissed and I couldn't control my nerves. As I exited the elevator, I brushed past people who were getting off as well. I noticed a couple of people lingering in the entrance area, and for some reason, I felt eyes staring at me. People whispered to one another, and others just stood there looking at me as if I was crazy. It was so obvious they knew who I was, and about the situation with Ra, that it left a weird feeling.

As long as I've lived in this building, I never knew anyone noticed Ra and I until this incident happened. Newspapers stated I got shot and that Ra was the person who shot me. Now people thought Ra was beating on me, because of all these lies that were spread over the news.

During the time I was in the hospital, I was questioned by police, asking if Ra was the one who shot me. I never answered any questions and told them to speak with my lawyer. They discovered later that we were a couple and didn't bother to ask any more questions. I knew people judged me because of the situation, but I didn't care. Screw whoever felt a way about us.

I walked through the main entrance as if I wasn't bothered by the comments that people made. But deep down inside, I couldn't wait to get out of the building. I walked to my car and noticed orange envelopes on the windshield wipers. "Dang," I said, as I smacked my forehead. I forgot to put the car in the parking lot that night. Being that I was in the hospital, I had no access to move my car. Another issue added to my problems.

I kindly took the tickets and placed them in the glove department. I turned the radio on to 105.1, in time for the Breakfast Club. It was one of my favorite radio shows. I guess this would play on my way to the Island. I got to the Island in no time. I beat the traffic, so I was early.

It was 10 a.m., and I didn't know the schedule for visiting hours. I had never come across a situation where I had to visit an inmate, but I always heard the stories. I did not think in a million years I would have to live it. I noticed a bridge that had to be crossed, and saw a booth nearby. Several cars stopped at the box to get permission to drive through.

I drove up to the booth, where a guy was sitting inside. He was a correction officer. He looked at me weird as I rolled down my window. "Hello, I'm here to see Rasheem Mills." The officer looked and started busting out laughing. I didn't know what was so funny, so I just looked at him and waited until he stopped laughing. "Excuse me..." I said, as he continued to laugh. It had to be 2 minutes until I got a response.

"Ma'am you have to park your car in the parking lot and the bus will bring you over the bridge." All he had to do was say that instead of laughing the whole time. I was so mad and confused about this visiting crap, because I had no clue what to do. Wiping the sweat from under his eyes from laughing so hard, he pointed in the direction of the parking lot. I noticed the lot when I first entered. "Make a U-turn so you can go to the parking lot," the officer said. "Ok sir," I said. He laughed again shaking his head.

I did as I was instructed and made a U-turn. I found a parking space towards the back, near a gate. When I parked my car, I saw the bus coming. "Shit!" I said, as I turned the car off and hurried out. I started walking fast so I wouldn't miss the bus, and noticed that there was a line of people waiting for the bus.

"Whew!" I said. I slowed down because speed walking made my back hurt. My back started to ache bad, but I was able to make the bus. I entered the bus with a whole lot of people. Some stood up, and others had a seat. There were a lot of young girls on the bus and girls with kids. "Miss, Miss," the bus driver said. Breaking my focus on not having a seat, I turned around facing him. "Yes," I said, with a puzzled look. "$2.50," he said. "Huh!" I said confused. "You have to pay once you get on the bus, its $2.50." he said with an attitude.

Oh, I said to myself, I checked my pockets and realized my wallet was in the car. I only had my car keys. "Shit!" I said, "Can I run to the car and grab my wallet, I left it." He looked at me like the officer did when I first entered, but he didn't laugh. "Miss you have to pay or get off my bus!" he said. My facial expression could have told him off, but I ignored the rude comment. Before I could say anything, a girl said she'd pay as she entered the bus. I turned around to a young girl with her son on her hip.

She swiped the metro card twice, and the man closed the door. "Thank you," I said looking at her. "No problem!" she said, as he continued to hold her baby on her hip. "I'll pay you back," I said to her, but she waved her hand, telling me not to worry about it. Since there weren't any seats on the bus, we had to stand until we got off.

"You're new at this huh?" the girl asked, holding her baby in her hand. "Yes I am, I don't know anything about these procedures," I said shaking my head. She smiled. She was a beautiful girl, and I could tell she was around 18 years old. "Do you have money to get your locker?" she asked. "No, I don't. You mean its more money involved? Oh boy," I said, shaking my head again. She reached in her pocket and gave me a quarter and a metro card. "Thank you, you don't have to," I said.

"No, I want to, it's not a big deal," she said. "I have plenty of metro cards, I'll be ok." she said smiling. I didn't want to take it, but I had no choice because I didn't have a way back. "Next time you will return the favor, I'm sure of it," she said smiling.

"Thanks," I said with a smirk. She nodded her head as she rocked her baby to sleep. Before you knew it, we'd reached the other side of the bridge. Everyone got up and were exiting off the bus. "Next time you better have money," the bus driver said as I was getting off.

I looked at him rolling my eyes and walked away.

I reached the place where the lockers were and put my keys inside. "All ID'S must be out before you get searched. Everything must be in lockers, no phones, keys, bags, or beepers," the correction officer announced, as everybody put everything in his or her lockers. I stood on the line while the correction officer searched IDs. I was so cold I couldn't wait to get in. I tapped my pocket. Oh shit! Did I leave my ID on the bus? I couldn't remember if I had it on me or if I left it in the car. My mind was just all over the place. I know before I left the house I put my ID in my back pocket. Damn! I thought.

I reached the correction officer, and I told him I had just lost my ID. Is there another way I could get in?" He looked at me like the bus driver, and the guard did earlier. He shook his head no. "Sir come on, I need to be on this visit," I said pleading. "Please step to the side ma'am, you are holding up my line". I became furious. "How in the world did I lose my ID? What do I do now?" I said, walking away from the line. Tears had welled up in my eyes, because I didn't know what else to do. I felt myself breathing hard again, so I leaned against the lockers to catch my breath.

I couldn't turn around now, I thought I know there has to be another way. I knew I needed my ID. The line was thinning, and there left one correction officer standing. Maybe if I could explain, he would help me. I dried my tears, and I walked back over to the correction officer. He looked at me with his arms crossed and waited to see what I had to say. "Sir, I'm sorry to bother you, but can you tell me about the visiting hours, so I know when to come back?" I asked still having little tears in my eyes.

"Miss it runs from different last names, and there will be different days. Today's visits are from M-Z. The next visiting day for M-Z will be Thursday, from 9 to 1." he said, still with his arms crossed. "And what time does the visit end today?" I asked. "Today's visit ends the same time, 9 to 1". "So you mean to tell me it's nothing else I can do? I lost my ID, and it will probably be a while before I could get another one." I said, hoping he felt some sympathy. "I need to see him," I said complaining. However, this time I started breathing heavy again.

"Miss calm down," he said unfolding his arms. I took a deep breath and tried calming my nerves. I put my hand on my back, because the pain started to come back again. Being that it was so cold, my hands were getting numb, and my back ached. "I'm sorry sir, but you don't know what kind of day I had. I'm mad I missed this visit, because I really can't miss it."

"Are you calm?" he asked. "Yes, I'm better, my nerves are calming down. Thank you, sir," I said. He was loosening up alittle and this time had more compassion. "Whom did you come to see?" he asked. It was kind of weird that he asked me that, because I felt like he was flirting. "My boyfriend," I said, "Boyfriends name?" "Does it matter? If you can't help me, there's no need to know." I said with a little attitude.

"I am trying to help you miss, that is why I need to know his name," he said, sarcastically. I looked at him squinting my eyes, because I felt like he was too nosy. "Rasheem Mills," I said giving him a strange look. "Ra? You Ra's girl?" he asked. I looked at him puzzled and wasn't sure if I was supposed to say yes or no.

"Yes," I said, giving him a hesitant answer. "It's me, Reggie!" "Reggie?" I asked unsure of who he was. "Yeah, I'm Ra's brother, he didn't tell you about me?" Then suddenly it hit me. Reggie was one of Ra's childhood friends, who Ra always mentioned from his childhood memories. I remember him telling me they lost contact, but I thought he was in Atlanta.

"Oh my gosh! Yes! Reggie, you look so much different from your pictures." "Yes, Tye! Ra told me you were coming, that's why I took this post," he said rubbing his hands together.

"Are you serious?" I asked. I was happy, and I felt relieved. "Omg, Reggie the day I had, you wouldn't even understand," I said shaking my head. After all, I was going to get my visit.

I can imagine the day you had. You would have had another bad day. I looked at him confused on what he was talking about. "What do you mean?" I asked looking confused. Someone came up here for Ra, but I wasn't sure if it was you. So, I asked her name, and it wasn't you, so I told her that there were no visits today. OH, hell no, I thought to myself. He called his side chick to come up here to see him. "What! Are you kidding me?" I asked with anger.

"Look Tye, this is why I made sure to be here and not another coworker. I know you not a dumb woman and Ra knows you aren't. So, to avoid any misunderstandings, I had to be blunt with you. Trust me, he is not trying to hurt you. Remember this is all over the news. He wouldn't allow another person to come see him if it wasn't you, "Reggie said with a serious face. I felt like an idiot and didn't know which way to lean, but I just ate it up, because right now it was about Ra.

"Your right! I get it." Deeps thoughts ran through my mind and I felt a pain in my heart. It is crazy to say, but I was so worried about him, that I didn't care about anything else. I knew this would be a battle that we would have to fight together. I knew that this was going be a long journey and alot to deal with.

"Meet me over there near the gate" he said, pointing towards the bus stop. "And I will be there to get you," he said, as he walked up a ramp leading inside the building. I walked over to the gate he pointed to and waited for him to come. It was cold. I tried not to think about the cold air. However, as the wind blew, it stung my face. Within a few seconds, I saw him walk out. He pulled open the gate, and I walked inside.

We went inside the building for the searching process. There were two metal detectors and people on the line waiting to be processed. I was able to go before the people in the line. I felt bad, but I needed to get through. "Take off your boots and walk through," he said. I did as I was instructed to do. I ambled through the metal detector and grabbed my boots once I walked through.

We then walked to a room that said OBCC. I was not sure what that stood for, so ignored the letters. There was a girl behind the desk, who also was a correction officer. I noticed people in the lobby being seated. "Hey Tash, can you log her in for me?" he asked smiling at her. She looked me up and down without cracking a smile. I was not sure what her attitude was about, but I threw shade right back with my facial expression.

Reggie stood behind her as he watched her log me in. She had to input my name, date of birth, and whether or not I've ever visited an inmate before. Once I answered all of her questions, I had to put my finger on a digital screen, for fingerprinting. I then had to stand back and take a picture. "Say cheese," she said, giving a phony smile. I just looked with an attitude, as she snapped my photo. She then printed a paper out of the machine, with a picture of me and handed it to me. "Good looking Tash," he said touching her shoulder.

Reggie walked around and told me I'd have to wait there for a bus. "You mean I have to get on another bus and pay again?" I asked out of frustration. He laughed." Nah, they have to take you to OBCC. OBCC is where Ra is the located. From this point you are ok, but in the future, make sure you have your ID. Next time I cannot do this for you," Reggie said grinning, as he shook his head.

"Oh, my gosh Reggie! You are such a lifesaver. I appreciate this," I said hugging him. "You are welcome. I will be waiting for you on your way out ok?" he said. "Yes, thanks again". Within minutes they called out for the bus. I was already the first person on the line and walked outside to a tan school bus. I showed the man my picture ID card and sat in the front of the bus.

For some reason, the bus gave me the chills. It felt like I was the one going to jail. I just closed my eyes because I could not imagine what Ra was experiencing. There were only a few of us on the bus, and I could not believe how big the jail was. Everything around me looked strange, from the trees to the surroundings areas. Whatever building I saw looked weird and old. I just shook my head in disbelief and became nervous about the whole situation.

We made it to OBCC building. As I was exiting off the bus, people were coming out of the building, waiting to get on the bus. We walked towards a locked door and had to wait for the guard to open it. It was freezing outside, and my lips were chapped. I was surrounded by so much water, I felt like I was wading in the water.

The door clicked, and the guard opened it to let us in. "If you have any packages you need to leave for an inmate, please step to the left," the officer said as we entered inside. The few people that were on the bus all had packages and stepped to the left. I stayed on the line and proceeded to get searched. I had to go through the whole procedure again, including taking off my boots and walking through the metal detector.

"Please stand behind the curtain," she said. I stood behind the curtain, and she told me to lift up my pants legs and pull down my socks. I also had to lift my top up and pull my bra from under and shake. "Do you have any piercings?" she asked. I shook my head no. I was disturbed by the procedure of getting searched. "Put your boots back on and wait until your name is called."

There was so much I had to go through to see Ra. I hoped I did not have to do this for the rest of my life. I cannot believe it takes all this time to see somebody, I thought to myself, as I waited in the waiting area. It was a good while until they called me. It did not matter at this point. I just wanted to see him.

CHAPTER 12

Entering through the sliding doors, I noticed colorful tables of blue and red. It looked like a kindergarten classroom, especially the tables. I walked towards the Correction Officer and gave her my slip. "3rd table," she said. I counted the tables, and I was at a blue table. I did not understand why she did not just say the blue table but whatever I said, as I walked towards the little blue table. I faced the high window, and stared out in front of me. I folded my hands together patiently waiting for Ra.

I heard a buzzing sound, and I turned around to look. There he was, his facial hair neatly trimmed and a dark fade. He wore a green suit and tan slippers. For some reason I became nervous. My body was shaking, and chills ran through me. I do not know if it was from excitement or what, but I do know I was excited. As I slowly stood up, his arms widened with a smirk on his mouth.

Ra reached out, and hugged me. He squeezed me so tight. I tried not to yell from the pain in my back, and just ignored it because I did not want to let him go. "Damn! Babe you looking good" he said, looking me up and down. He was giving me a look like he was ready to do me, and I gave him the same look back. As we sat down, he looked and kept staring at me. "What's wrong?" I asked "Nothing, I am just happy you are ok, and you look good," he said. I knew he was worried about my back, but I did not want to talk about that. My focus was all on him.

"Baby I missed you so much. You do not know what kind of day I had trying to see you" I said smiling, as he touched my chin, lifting it up to kiss me on the lips. "Keep your hands to yourself," the guard said. I broke out of my moment of bliss and came back to reality.

"Baby how you been? Are you ok? What is happening?" I said, asking him 21 questions. He held his head down and looked back at me. "Tye, how is your back, are you ok?" Ra asked, ignoring my questions. I hated when he asked me a question on top of my questions. However, I just answered him.

"Babe I am fine, I do not want to discuss that," I said, putting my head down. I was kind of embarrassed because people thought Ra shot me intentionally. "I know how you feel babe. I was just so stressed, because you know I would never put you in a compromising situation. I would do anything to protect you" he said looking at me.

"I am so happy to see you are walking. This whole time I had visions that you were in a wheelchair. I had no idea you were walking. So, this made my day Tye. You do not know," he said feeling relieved. "I know, I know babe," I said. He touched my face, and I grabbed his hands. We had a little moment of silence.

I guess no one told him that I could walk and this whole time he thought I was paralyzed. I know he was losing his mind in here, I thought to myself. How Ra worried about me, I worried about him. Repeatedly Ra said the same thing over and over. "I'm so happy you ok" as he touched my face.

"It feels good seeing you babe," he said smiling at me. "It sure does!" I said blushing. "Being locked up with these dudes is crazy. I missed you, Tye. You know I love to see your hair like that" he said.

I started to grin. It felt like he was trying to ignore his surroundings and talk positive. It had been almost a month since we last saw each other.

"Tye I need a favor from you. You're the only one I can trust as of right now" he said. I was surprised because he never asked me for anything. "Babe I am always here, wassup?" I asked, waiting to hear what he had to say. "I need you to reach out to somebody named, Michael Bennett. He is a lawyer, and I need you to tell him my situation," Ra said, with a serious look on his face. "Where is he located?" I asked. "He is near the building of Mills Construction. It is a grey building, and it says, Mr. Bennett on the door. He is located on the second floor and has his own law firm," Ra said explaining the details. Mills construction was Ra's business that he owned. "Ok," I said. "Also, I need you to go to my office, and get the briefcase in the closet,"

"When you get the briefcase, let me know you have it and make sure you lock my office door. When you come up here Thursday, I will tell you what I want you to do with the briefcase." "Ok," I said. Listening to the way he was saying it, I knew it was very secretive. "Tye! Don't tell anybody about anything I tell you, and never discuss anything over the phone," he said. "Ok, Ra you know I am not like that." "I know, but sometimes you have to remind a person of what not to do," he said.

"Also, babe I need some clothes. I need underwear that are white, plain white socks, a black or white pair of pumas, that can't be any more than $40.00 and some grey thermals. I also need a $100 a week on commissary, and it has to be in before I go to commissary" he said. "Babe before you leave or before the day ends, make sure you put some money on my books." he said, giving me the details on what he needed.

I was confused, because I did not know how I was going to put money in his commissary with no money. "Babe, I left my wallet in the car". I said. "Cool, so download an app on your iPhone called Jpay. Put my DIN number in, and my name will pop up. Then you put the amount of money to transfer into my account. I will get it within minutes" Ra said explaining everything to me. For some reason I just thought he knew too much.

I was not sure if he went through this experience before or if someone told him about it. I did not want to ask or find out. "I got it," I said smirking. "Ra," I said softly. He looked at me, tilting his head to the side. "Yes, babe?" "Before I forget, I want to tell you I will stay by your side, I am not going anywhere." This time tears came into my eyes and started to drip down. As the tears dripped, Ra wiped them away, as I wiped the other side of my face. "I know babe," he said.

For a second, we were in another stage of silence. I wanted to know what happened that night, but I knew he did not want to discuss it. So I figured the best thing was not to ask. Within moments he said something funny and I began to laugh. We were ourselves again, talking about everything. From the first time we met to old stories.

"You were so cocky, I could not take you," I said. "Yeah, but my cockiness got you in my bed; the first night did it not?" he asked smirking. "That was because I thought I was going to be over with you," I said laughing. We laughed, giggled and talked about everything. Before you knew it, the visit was over. I almost forgot where I was for a second.

It was bittersweet. I did not want to leave, but I was so happy I saw Ra. They called his name, and I got up to hug him. To my surprise, Ra kissed me on the lips, leaving his tongue in my mouth. He then squeezed my butt not wanting to let go. I drifted off into another place and again didn't realize my surroundings.

I instantly fell into that blurr stage of mind and wanted more of Ra's hands all over me. "Hey... hey, time to go" the guard said with an attitude. I was not too fond of the way she looked at me but, she mad. He looked at me with those eyes, and I knew what that meant.

Once he entered the closing door, I couldn't see him anymore. I know I said I am going to be here, but this shit is very painful. "Damn," I said, walking towards the exit of the visiting room. Just like that, Ra was gone. I thought about the process of going back home and didn't want to remind myself. An hour visit felt like crap. I just needed to do what he told me to do.

On the ride home, I was curious to know if Ra had been there before, based on everything else he told me. I figured maybe Reggie told him about everything else. Ra knew a lot of information regarding the jail process. I am not sure if he's dealt with this experience in the past, but something did not sit right. It was strange that he had a lawyer working near him. I could understand now why Ra didn't want anybody in his business.

I also wondered about the briefcase and what was in it. However, I did not want to ask too many questions. I was the only person he could trust. So many thoughts triggered in my head causing me to wonder. Especially about the female who came up to see him. I knew I was just being silly and overthinking things. I did know that I missed him dearly though and prayed he'd be home soon. Only the Lord knows the truth.

As I drove, I prayed all the way home, praising God and talking to him. I knew he understood what I was going through. I knew I had to catch up with him and thought about attending church. I even thought about the miscarriage and how would life have turned out, if I did not have one? I still feel some way about that.

I even mentioned my mother to God and the memories I shared. How I missed her dearly and prayed she'd made it to heaven. At times I wish she was here to hold me and pray together. However, this was something that I had to deal with and not walk away from. I had to walk with faith and get through this as a woman.

CHAPTER 13

"Good morning, how can I help you?" The receptionist asked. "Good morning, I am Tye Rene, I am here to see Mr. Bennett," I said softly with a smile. She smiled back and gave me a sweet look. She was a dark-skinned woman, with a beautiful complexion. She was naturally beautiful and wore a natural look. When she smiled, her teeth were bright white, but I noticed a little red lipstick on the top of her teeth. But she was still naturally beautiful.

She picked up her phone and dialed Mr. Bennett's number. "Hello you have someone here to see you" she spoke softly on the phone. Within seconds she hung up. "Tye, he will be with you shortly, please have a seat," she said. "Thank you," I said walking away. I walked over to the empty seating area near the window.

I sat down and pulled my phone out. I noticed I had a text message from Kim. "Hey let's go out tonight for dinner" with an emoji of her blowing a kiss. "Ok great! I will see you tonight," I texted back. Within moments she texted back, "Tony's Roma's." I texted her back with a wink.

I had not been around Kim or Tania in a while. I called once in a while, but sometimes I just wanted to be left alone. I had been stressing about dealing with Ra's situation, so it was hard for me to have a life. It was hard for me to talk about everything that was happening. This was something different I had to deal with, and I did not think anyone could understand. However, one thing Kim always did, was make sure I was doing good by always checking up on me.

"Hello, Tye! I looked up and saw a dark, built, tall guy. He was muscular and a very handsome man. Moreover, for some reason, I did not picture Mr. Bennett looking this fine. "Yes, hi how are you doing?" I asked getting up. He reached out his hand giving me a handshake. "I am good, please come this way," he said. He pointed towards the back entrance, and I followed in that direction.

I entered a large room with a big window. The window's view exposed the Brooklyn Bridge. His desk sat near the large window and had two seats in front. "Please have a seat," he said, as he closed his office door. I sat in the seat that faced him. He then came around and sat behind his desk. "So, what can I do for you? "he asked, taking a sip out of his Starbucks coffee.

"Yes, Mr. Bennett, I am here because my boyfriend sent me to see you, Rasheem Mills". "Oh yes, my man Ra. Is everything ok?" he asked with a concerned look on his face. I shook my head no. "No, everything is not ok," I said, sounding a little sad. He looked at me taking another sip of his coffee. "Mr. Mills is being charged with murder" Mr. Bennett spat his coffee back into his cup. "Excuse me," he said placing the cup on the table. I could not even say another word, I just looked at him. Mr. Bennett shook his head in disbelief, and I could tell he was shocked. "I have known Ra for a long time, and murder does not sound like him at all," he said. I could not even speak any more about it, because it still bothered me.

"When is his next visiting hours?" he asked, putting his hands on his chin. "Next Monday, from 9 to 1," I said. I could tell he wanted to speak more to Ra rather than me. "Ok, that is good for me. When you speak to him, tell him I will be there on Monday!" he said. "Here is my number, call me if anything," he said, giving me a business card. I took the card and put it in my purse. "Thank you," I said. "No, thank you," he said. As I got up, he got up as well. I walked towards the door. "Don't worry I got this," Mr. Bennett said, putting his hand on my shoulder. "I hope so," I said silently, smiling.

I had researched Mr. Bennett, and found he was a good lawyer. He had represented many murder cases and had beaten them. Mr. Bennett was also a costly lawyer. I did not know how expensive, but I knew Ra had a plan. Being that Ra was out of work and business was slow, I knew our funds were tight. I had enough money saved just for a rainy day, so I knew we'd be good as a as lawyer fees.

"Well thank you, Mr. Bennett, I look forward to hearing from you," I said, leaving out of his office. "Likewise," he said, as I continued to wait for the elevator. I thought to myself and wondered, Ra knew so many people who cared about him. People had reached out to me concerned about the news they heard, and offered nothing but love and support. It was well appreciated, because no one said anything negative about him. That was a good feeling to have.

The next step was to get the briefcase from the office. I reached the first floor to Ra office and opened his door. I admired how neat and clean it was. There were two cabinets, one that was large and the other was smaller. The first cabinet I searched was the big locker and didn't see anything. Then the smaller cabinet which had a key to open it. Ra you did not tell me about a key, I said to myself. So, from the set of keys I grabbed from the house, I tried all of them. Thankfully one of the keys worked, and I opened the closet.

There was the suitcase. I tried lifting up the suitcase and it was so heavy. I felt pressure in my back and it started to hurt, so I put it back down. Now Ra knows my back is messed up, I thought to myself. I then tried lifting it with two hands and placed it on the floor. I did not want anyone to see me struggle with the suitcase. So, I looked around to see how could I get this out without being noticed.

A traveling bag was under Ra's table, which was a lifesaver. The traveling bag had wheels, which was even better. "Thank God!", I said to myself. I pulled the bag to where the briefcase was, and with deep breaths, put it inside. It hurt like hell rolling this out of the building, but I managed to get it out of the office. I made sure the doors and everything were locked.

After leaving Ra's office, later on that day, I had to finish going through therapy. I still had a once a week therapy session, that I had to complete for three months. My doctor said I was healing up good. I felt relieved about my back, because I was still self-conscious about what took place. Afterward, I headed to the salon to get pampered. Lord knows I needed it. I had been so depressed about Ra, while dealing with my issues as well. I hadn't cared about my beauty or anything else.

I thought I was over the fact of me losing my baby, but for some reason, it kept coming back to memory. I tried to block it out of my head and use different things to distract me, but time from the time it would come up. I decided that the salon would distract me from just being home crying all day. So, I decided to get my hair done to keep my mind off everything.

CHAPTER 14

Shic is one of my favorite salons in Brooklyn on myrtle ave. I've known them for years, and they were professional at what they did. They always made their clients feel welcome. I could talk to them when dealing with a bad day or situation, and for some reason they made me forget about the kind of day I was having. Their personalities were sweet, and they were so down to earth.

The shop was set up with nails, hair, and makeup. They were amazing at their work, and I loved every bit of their work. I knew I was going to be late meeting Kim and Tania tonight, but it was on the way to downtown Brooklyn anyway. "Hey, Portia" I greeted my stylist, with kisses and a hug. She greeted me back with a hug and held it for a moment. "I am so sorry to hear about what's been happening to you," she whispered in my ear.

At that moment I wanted to break down in her arms. Her hug was so sincere, that I didn't want to let go. I needed a hug, and the comfort of her support made me feel safe. "I will not ask any questions, but I will keep Ra and you in my prayers," she said, kissing me on the cheek.

Tears slid down as she let go and she wiped them off. I smiled because I could not even talk at that moment. I just cried. It just felt as if she was part of me and what I was going through. I saw the tears in her eyes, but she didn't dare let them drop. Her goal was to keep me uplifted. "Thanks, Portia," I said, re-wiping the tears that kept falling. "You're welcome, now look at that head. It needs a lot of work," she said laughing, rubbing her hands through my hair. "Girl only if you knew," I said shaking my head.

We walked towards the back, and there were so many people, it was kind of crowded. Some waited under the dryer, and some waited to be washed. Others were there for sewn in weaves. As I walked past, I saw a couple of eyes looking and smiled. I knew they wanted to know and be nosey, but it didn't bother me. I just pretended no one was there.

"Sit here," Portia said, ready to wash me. I sat at the sink for my hair to be washed, while she got supplies for my hair. She covered me up with a washing cape, and lightly put my head back against the sink. "Umm," I whispered, as she washed and massaged my head. It was relaxing and put me at ease. For some reason, my scalp was very tender, maybe from stress. But as Portia washed and massaged, it felt much better, and I was more relaxed.

Portia then deep conditioned my hair and sat me under the dryer. I dried for about 30-35 minutes and then she put me in her chair. It was already 7:30 pm and I still had to put some pieces in my hair. I didn't have time to get my pedicure, but I got a manicure. My manicure was being done as Portia was sewing some pieces in my hair. "Where are you?" came a text message from Kim. At this time, it was 8:15pm and I was already 15 minutes late. "I will be there in about another 15 minutes," I texted back. Hopefully, I'd finish in 15 minutes, since Portia was still curling me up. "Smh!" Kim texted back. However, I ignored her.

Within 10 minutes Portia was done. She curled me all up and also made enough time to make up my face. I felt like myself again. I figured when I got home, I would take some sexy pictures for Ra. "Thank you, Portia!" I said, as I looked at myself in the mirror. I reached in my bag and pulled out $300.00. She gave it back to me and said, "next time". "Thanks Portia," I said softly, "Anytime Tye, I got you," she said. We embraced each other with another hug and kissed. "See you next time," she said. "For sure," I said waving good-bye, walking out the door.

As I got in my car, Kim was calling. "Hello," I said, as I sat in the car. "Girl, where are you?" she asked with an attitude. For some reason, I almost snapped back, but I didn't because I was in a good mood. "I am on my way now!" I said. Without her saying anything else she hung up. I instantly got mad, and I knew I had to tell her about herself. I didn't know what was eating Kim up, but she had never acted like that before.

It took me no more than 5 minutes to reach Tony Roma's, and I was so lucky to find suitable parking. "Dang," I said to myself as I walked inside. It was crowded, and I couldn't spot Kim and Tania anywhere. However, it just so happened Kim noticed me and waved her hand. I pointed towards Kim to let the waiter know that I'd found my party. She nodded and smiled.

"Hey girl," I said, reaching out to hug her. However, I could tell she was still upset and gave me a half-ass hug. "Tania!" I said, letting go of Kim. "Hey, girl you look so pretty, love the hair," Tania said, reaching out to hug me. "Thank you, Tania," I said smiling. I could tell they had been drinking, especially Tania. "Did you ladies eat yet?" I asked looking at the menu. "No! we were waiting for you" Kim said, maintaining her attitude. I could not take any more smart remarks from her. "What is your problem, Kim? You are giving me so much attitude, for what?" I asked, folding my arms together.

"You are my problem! I invite you out, and you take a year and a day to get here. Why must you think it is always about you?" Kim asked. "First of all Kim, yes, I took a minute to get here. But only because I also had a hair appointment. I am sorry she could not rush me to meet you here on time, but I don't know who the fuck you're talking to!" I said, with so much anger. "Oo come on yall, it is not that serious. We all here now, so it is no need to be arguing," Tania said, trying to calm both of us down.

At this point neither one of us were listening to Tania, because at that moment we kept going back and forth. "Tye you are so self-centered, this is why I need to stay away from your selfish ass. Ever since that shit happened, you call yourself avoiding me" Kim said. "I am selfish? How am I selfish Kim? Whenever your ass needs something, I'm always there. So don't ever call me selfish!" I said, yelling out loud. "Tye!, you are selfish. It is always about you and Ra. You revolve your life around Ra. This is why…" Kim said, not wanting to finish the rest of her sentence. "This is why what Kim? Say it! We are all adults. What?" I asked yelling. "This is why Ra got another bitch going up there to see him. You think you his only bitch?" Kim asked yelling out.

My ears went deaf from what Kim had just told me. I was beyond deaf, I was over it. "Damn, it took an argument for you to throw some shit like this in my face? Kim how about I knew he had another bitch going up there to see him," I said with a smirk. "And if you didn't know, the bitch that is going up there to see him, Kareem fucks her sister.

Now before you air my shit out, make sure you research your own shit…" I said getting up. "And oh yea, I begged Kareem to marry your ass because he knew about you fucking Ice…" I said looking dead at her. I was lying because I did not have a comeback after she had told my truth. "Fuck you, Tye! You have always been jealous, ever since Kareem proposed to me. You wish it were you." Kim said getting up.

We were arguing not realizing we were in the restaurant. "Jealous, of you Kim? Wow, never that. I was so excited for your engagement, probably happier than you." I had to laugh because Kim was saying some crazy stuff. I was shocked because Kim had never acted like that. I didn't know what happened, but she took it to the next level.

"It is crazy how you think so low of me. There must be something within yourself that might has you jealous of me," I said.

We were actually in each other faces, as if it was about to go down. Tania jumped up in between us and told us to calm down. "And yes, I was avoiding you Kim, because neither one of you bitches knows what I am going through..." I said, saying it so nasty. I knew Tania felt some way, but I didn't care. Forget the both of them. I grabbed my coat off the seat and walked through the crowd of people. People were staring at me, and I was so embarrassed that I had to go through that.

The nerve of Kim, thinking somebody was jealous over her engagement. She didn't even know I actually help picked out her ring and everything. How could she have thought I was avoiding her on purpose, when I had to deal with all this shit. All these thoughts ran through my head. I was furious to hear about somebody going up there to see Ra.

That tore me up because, I was home worrying about this shit and he had bitches going to see him. Reggie warned me other females were going up there. Maybe he warned me just in case I bumped into one of them on the visiting floor. Who knows, but I did not care because I was sticking by his side. I cried out of anger. "God help me, forgive me for the nasty mouth I had towards my friends." I didn't want that to go down, but I was hurting at the time. I just cried in the car for a moment, trying to pull myself together.

Breaking my prayer, my phone rang. I thought it was Kim, but I saw an unknown number. "Hello?" An inmate at Rikers Island is trying to reach you. Without letting the operator finish, I pressed one. "Hello, hey girl wassup?" he asked sounding all cool. "Hi," I said dryly. "Why you sound upset?" he asked. I wanted to say something about that bitch going up there, but I did not want to cause him any stress, so I left it alone. "No reason, I am just a little tired," I said. "Oh ok, how was your day?" he asked. "It was cool. I went to go see your lawyer today, he said he would see you on Monday." "Good stuff, thanks, babe. Did you go to my office to check on things?" "Yes, I did it, babe. Everything was going well." That was just another way of telling him I got the briefcase from his office. "Thanks, babe…"

We talked a little while on the phone. Ra made me feel a little better about my argument with Kim. He always had a way of calming me. We had a good conversation about many things. Ra had an uplifted spirit, and he didn't seem stressed at all. He was normal, and I liked hearing that he was in a good state of mind. "You have 60 seconds remaining," the lady said. "I hate this part," I said. I started to get a little sad, because I didn't want to get off the phone, but I knew I had to.

"I will call you tomorrow," Ra said. "Ok, I love you," we said at the same time, and that was the end of the call. By that time, I was already parked in front of my building. I had made it home while speaking to him on the phone. Damn, I missed Ra a lot, I thought to myself.

As I entered the building, I had to bring the duffle bag inside. I was able to drag the bag without struggling. I looked into my mailbox and grabbed some mail. I smiled because, I received a letter and card from Ra. My heart started pounding. I didn't know if it was good or bad, but I could not wait to read them.

Once I entered my apartment, I pulled the duffle bag and put it in my closet. I wasted no time taking my clothes off and running a hot bath. I lit some candles and dimmed the lights. I pictured this as a date night for Ra and I. As my body settled in the bath, I was consumed by the temperature of the water and was in my comfort zone. My hair was pinned up, and I pampered my face with a cucumber facial.

I then grabbed the card, so anxious to read it. *"Happy Anniversary." Hey babe, I usually don't write cards, but I wanted to wish you a Happy 4th year anniversary. Love Ra.*

Aww, I smiled as I closed the card, remembering today was our anniversary. I couldn't believe I forgot. I was so wrapped up in the argument with Kim, that I didn't even say Happy Anniversary to him. I laughed to myself, because I was flattered that he remembered. I then opened the letter, which wasn't long. I knew Ra didn't like writing much, but every word counted.

"Tye!

Wassup babe…? How is everything? You know I do not write much, but there is something that I have to get off my chest. I want to say I am sorry I left you out there. I am sorry I disappointed you. Never wanted this to happen, but I know things happen for a reason. Also, if I forgot to tell you, I want to apologize for putting you in this situation. I may not know what will happen today or tomorrow, but if you were to leave me, I would understand. I would not hold it against you. You do not have to suffer for my selfish ways. I love you, Tye. Hopefully, I'll see you soon.

Love Ra…

Tears fell through the cucumber facial. "Damn," I said out loud. "Is this happening? I never thought about leaving him because we were in this together. Despite of what he did in the past, I would never leave Ra alone in this situation. Especially with him feeling like this. I knew we would beat this. "We will beat this," I said to myself. "We will win," I said. I continued to soak my body in the warm bath.

My soap dissolved and it just left the clear water. I just sat thinking about what was next. I told myself to be strong for him, so that was what I was going to do. If he thought I was leaving him, he thought wrong. I will be here to the end, I thought to myself.

CHAPTER 15

Ra…

Dripping sweat, he jumped up to a sound of a gun. All the lights were out, and he could barely see anything. Ra sat up in his bed with his hands covering his head. He grabbed the toilet paper that was on the side of his bed, and wiped the sweat that ran down his face. "Damn," he said, wiping the sweat from his face.

It had been an on and off thing with Ra not getting sleep. He suffered from nightmares about that night of New Year's Eve, and tried putting pieces together. Every dream he had, he wrote it down on a piece of paper to match everything together. It helped him a lot with his memory to try and grasp what took place that night.

Ra pulled the book from under his pillow and wrote down what he had dreamt of. He made a timeline from each dream he had, and wrote it in his book. Each time Ra had a dream it was a story, but it was the same. Tye, Kim, and Tania were at the front entrance, and that is where Tania was shot. Kareem was stopping Ra from fighting Toast. Ra knew that was not true, but this was the dream he had the night before and wrote it down. He didn't understand why it had to be Tania and Toast, but for some reason, it was a sign.

Ra also dreamt that a guy was pulling on Tye. Tye was telling him to stop, but he kept grabbing her. Tye didn't know the guy, but the guy must have seen her with Ra. He didn't know what it meant, but he knew he would have to talk to Mr. Bennett about this. There were visions that were coming back to Ra and it felt like déjà vu. Ra had finally figured out his dream.

It was a set-up by one of his friends, and he had a feeling that it could have been Toast and Tania. It was kind of silly to jump to conclusions off of a dream, but he knew it had to be true. Something was not right, and he had to figure it out. Ra laid back down thinking about that night. He could not remember everything, only what his dreams told him. Ra had to discuss the matter with Michael. Ra thought really hard for a moment and drifted off back to sleep.

Michael knew a lot about the streets, and sought to find information regarding people Ra associated with. Michael lived a different lifestyle. He was known to be in the streets long ago and had a past as well. Michael had caught a murder case for two bodies at the age of 16. He was convicted of 2nd-degree murder, and had been sentenced to 25 years to life.

Michael grew up in a foster home with a group of boys in Newark, NJ. He was a troubled teen and hung around troubled teens as well. They called themselves Bad-ass. Nobody messed with them. They got into all kinds of things such as; drugs, robbery, and assault. However, Michael had a different mindset from the rest. Michael sold drugs, while his group of friends used them. He was not really into robbing people or beating them up, but if his friends got into confrontations, he'd help defend them.

One day in the summertime, the Bad-asses were up to no good and got into in a brawl. They were fighting another group of teens. Michael happened to see his friends fighting and ran over to jump in. Manny who was in Badass, was being jumped by two people. When Michael discovered that it was his friend, he started fighting with him.

Michael knew how to fight, and fought both guys off of Manny. Suddenly out of nowhere, Manny got up and stabbed one of the guys Michael was fighting. He repeatedly stabbed him in the stomach. The police came and broke up the brawl. Michael didn't realize the police were there and they grabbed Michael, throwing him on the floor. Several police came over and handcuffed Michael. Everybody ran, including the Badasses. Michael was the only one who was arrested from Badass.

Michael was taken in for questioning and interrogated. Michael didn't speak or answer any of the questions that the police were asking. He then discovered the boy that got stabbed was dead. Michael didn't have anything to do with the boy's stabbing. Being that he didn't answer any of the questions, they pinned the charge on him. Michael was arrested for murder. He called members from Badass for help, but none of them bothered to answer his phone calls.

Michael didn't have any visits from his friends or any help. He was alone and figured they didn't want any parts. Being that he didn't have any money for a lawyer, he was assigned a public defender to help him with his case. He still didn't mention anything about how the boy was stabbed, he kept it to himself. Michael didn't want to take it to trial because he didn't have any money. So, when he had to go to court, he copped out to 25 years to life, since he was charged as an adult.

At that age, Michael didn't know anything about the law or a defense. Being that he was so young, he didn't think anything of it and thought it was normal. However, he then decided that he was not going to rot for a crime he didn't commit. He knew he had to prove his innocence, the best way he knew how. He wound up reading up on law and learning his rights, while being locked up. It was three years later when Michael finally got an answer for his appeal. After he had his appeal hearing, Michael was a free man at 19.

The charges were dropped because they never found any evidence linking him. He prayed for that day and was able to turn his life around. He was motivated to help other people with their cases. Michael went on to get a GED and later attended college. He was able to receive his Bachelors in Criminal Justice, then attended Harvard Law school. Michael then received his Master's in Law. He later moved to New York, where he opened up his own small law firm. Then years later, he relocated to where Ra had first opened his business, which is how they first met. Michael is 33 years old now and a successful lawyer.

Later on, that day, Ra had a visit from Kareem. Kareem always made his way to see Ra. Ra also had other friends come and visit him as well. Ra was so popular and loved, that he always had a visit. He was usually booked all the way to the end of the month. It made Ra's day go by fast, and helped him maintain his composer.

"Kareem, wassup my guy?" Ra asked. Kareem stood up with a smile on his face. "Wassup Ra, I see you getting your weight up," Kareem said. They gave each other a dap and sat down. "Yeah, man there is nothing else to do but to work out," Ra said, holding his arms. "Anyways, wassup with you? What's new out there?" Ra asked, folding his hands. "Man, I'm managing, but it is not the same anymore," Kareem said, shaking his head. "Business is slow, and I am not into hustling anymore. I am trying to get a job," Kareem said, putting his head down.

"Yea I know what you mean, but you know you can try construction. I told you whenever you really want to work, you can work with me, "Ra said. Ra had given Kareem plenty of opportunities to come join his team. But Kareem was in the street life and didn't think the working field would be good for him.

"Yeah, I know, and I am considering that offer, "Kareem said." I need a change in my life Ra. Things are not the same and I really need to get my life together, "Kareem said". I understand and I could give you all the advice you need, "Ra said." But first thing is, while I'm in here take up some business courses and understand how the business world works. Then we can get you started with everything else, "Ra said." "Also, when you work for me, make sure you know I'm your boss," Ra said joking with Kareem. "Yeah ok man," Kareem said laughing. "Yeah you'll be good Kareem," Ra said.

"Another thing, most dudes are acting funny style, and I cannot trust a lot of people anymore." "Oh, word? Wassup with Toast? Last time I saw him was that night. I called him and everything, but he ignores my calls." Ra said.

"Man, Toast is acting funny style. I feel like knocking him out," Kareem said. Ra laughed shaking his head. "Come on Kareem, you can't do that," Ra said. Kareem looked at Ra with a serious face, and Ra knew he was not playing. "Ra, that dude Toast, I have not spoken to him at all. He has been ducking me, and I don't know why or wassup with him. I know shit does not feel right. I have to keep an eye on him." Kareem said.

"Dang, it is like that Kareem? I mean maybe he is going through something," Ra said. "Yeah, please Ra. Toast is bugging, that is all I am saying," Kareem said. "But when I see him I am knocking his ass out," Kareem said. They both started laughing. Ra knew Kareem knew something but didn't want to tell him. Ra assumed his dream could have been the truth.

"Anyways, how is Kim and the engagement going?" Ra asked, hitting Kareem on the hand. "Man, that's another thing," he said, shaking his head. "I should have waited to propose, because now she's pregnant. Kim is bugging out and aggravating me, but I am happy I am about to be a father," Kareem said. Ra's eyes widened as Kareem was telling him about his new bundle of joy.

"You about to be a father, that is a blessing Kareem," Ra said. "Tye never told me anything about Kim having a baby," Ra said, with a concerned look on his face. "Kim and Tye are not talking," Kareem said shaking his head. "Word? When did this happen?" Ra asked. "Man, I do not even know. But they are not talking, so Kim didn't tell Tye that she was pregnant," Kareem said.

Ra had a surprised look on his face, not believing what he just heard. He thought to himself, what could have happened to their friendship. He knew that was their business and it was not the best idea to bring it up.

Ra had an enjoyable visit with Kareem. They talked about everything and especially about his case. The visit was over, and they both had to part ways. "I'll see you soon," Kareem said, getting up to hug Ra. Their bond was more like brothers than friends. "Until next time," Ra said. Kareem sat back down and watched Ra go through the double doors.

Later on that day, Ra called Tye. "Hey babe, wassup with you?" he asked. "Heyyy! Babe, nothing much, I miss you" she said with excitement. "Miss you more, what are you doing?" he asked, with a grin on his face. "Nothing, just came home from picking you up some tops and washing your clothes. Thursday I will bring you your package" she said, smiling through the phone. "Oh ok! Babe you on point with everything huh?" he asked laughing. "Yup! I got everything covered for you," Tye said. "Aww, what would I do without you babe?" he asked and heard her chuckle through the phone.

"I appreciate you being here for me Tye, thanks, "Ra said." You lift up my spirits everyday, even though I can't see your face, "he said, expressing his feelings to her." I have been thinking alot about my life and both of our futures. Ra had started reading the bible and taking his religion seriously. He also said he had been praying and talking to God every day.

"He's the best man I have ever encountered. I know that God is a forgiving God," Ra said, and believed everything would be ok. "I know it," he said. "I apologize that I have not been there for you since the miscarriage," "I am sorry you had to deal with it alone, as well as my shortcomings as your man, "Ra said, still expressing himself to me." I am sorry I cheated on you and hid it from you," Ra continued, confessing his feelings over the phone.

"I needed to get it off of my chest, and I will tell you again once I see you. However, I wanted to tell you now," Ra said, as I listen to everything. I appreciate you in my life each day. Thankful you are here. This is not easy for one to deal with, especially a woman. However, thanks, Tye, "Ra said. For a moment there was silence.

As Ra confessed and admitted things to me, all I could do was listen and cry. I was so happy that he was able to speak his mind, because his apology meant so much to me. "Aww babe, you are welcome. I told you I am riding this out with you," I said. "Thank you for the apology. I know we never spoke about the miscarriage, but I beat myself up every day and God helped me through it. I knew you cheated, and someone came up there to visit you, but I didn't bring it up." I believed certain things needed to be addressed at a certain time in life. I believed that was the perfect timing to clear the air. "Remember babe, God has a reason for everything," I said, as the tears poured down my face. However, like He said, "Walk by Faith and not by Sight."

Ra could tell I had a little sadness in my voice and he knew I was about to cry again. There was a silence between the both of us. "Tye you still there?" he asked. "Uh huh," I said, and he already knew I was crying.

"Babe?" He said. "Yes Ra?" "Are you ok?" "Yes, I am ok. That was just a lot to hear and take in. I know it was not easy for you to express everything to me. But I am glad you were able to understand. We will work through this together."

Let me ask you a question I said. "Yes, Tye," Ra said, waiting for the question. "The night of the event, did you leave me to see another girl?" I asked. My heart beat so fast and I wished I'd never asked the question, but I did and had to know. "Yes, I did Tye. I broke it off with her though," he said. The phone was in a deep silence. But I was so happy that he didn't lie.

"I wanted to tell the truth, Tye," Ra said breaking my silence. "I'm here!" I said dryly. So, was she the one who came up there to see you?" I asked. Ra was silent, but I knew it was her before he could even respond. "60 more seconds," the operator said. "I guess it is time to go." "Babe, "you ok?" Ra asked. "Yes, I know the truth and I don't want to talk about it anymore. I will see you early tomorrow," I said. Before he could even get a word out, the phone clicked.

I was relieved and felt cleansed. Ra had never admitted his wrong doings. So for him to tell me, I knew he was changing. I smiled because after all this, I loved him even more. All was behind us, and I'd be able to move forward.

CHAPTER 16

It was 9:30 am, and I was waiting for the guards to come and check me in. I had to go through one more search, and I would have my visit with Ra. I made sure I was there early, just in case something happened. Ra and I were going to have an extended visit, because Reggie worked the visitation floor. Reggie had been a big help since Ra had been locked up.

Reggie made sure Ra was good with his packages and visits. Even though Reggie wasn't supposed to have any contact with an inmate, he managed to let me get away with certain things. Because of Reggie, I had alot of leniency with doing certain things. Due to Reggie being good friends with his lady captain, whatever information was delivered to her, she ignored. Thank God for Reggie.

"Hey Reg," I said, as I entered the double doors. He got up out of his seat and hugged me. "Everything good?" he asked, as we embrace with a hug. "Yes," I said. He nodded his head and took the slip out my hand. "Go sit by the wall in the corner," he said, pointing in the direction towards the wall. I slightly smiled and walked towards the corner. I waited patiently for Ra to come through the doors.

I thought to myself and wondered, what if I was on the other side? Would Ra be here for me? If only I could have stopped him that night. If only I could even remember that night. We would have never been in this shit. This is a depressing suicide zone. All these crazy thoughts came rushing through my head. I became so mad and sad at the same time that, tears started to pour down my face. Just the thought of this being our life messed me up.

It was so hard for me to deal with this, because I still hadn't accepted this life. It felt like I was living in a nightmare that I would never wake up from. Ever since this fatal nightmare occurred, I'd lost my appetite. I cried half of the night and day, as if it was ritual, I did every second of every day. The only time my spirit was lifted up was when I prayed, or spoke to Ra. Talking about stress, my stress damn near killed me. I'd never spoken about it to Ra, but I had a nervous breakdown a couple of times.

No one knew what I was going through. My family never really cared for Ra, so I never even spoke about it to them. Friends I did have, I lost. But I didn't even notice or care. Ever since I stopped talking to Kim, Tania hadn't even reached out to me. I thought that was weird, but I paid no attention to it. I was just numb to everything. I didn't care what happened at that time and tried keeping the negative thoughts out of my head.

My relationship with God was a strong bond. When you have faith, you can't have any stress. You have to believe God has you all the time. It wasn't that I didn't trust, but I had to completely trust him and everything he did. That's why I prayed so much, so I didn't have to feel this way. This was something that God could not pass me through, but to walk with me through it.

"Sexy, sexy babe," Ra said, walking up to me. I didn't even notice Ra walking up, that's how zoned out I was. I slowly got up snapping out of my mood, and reached out and gave Ra a hug. I held out my arms, and we hugged for a moment that felt like forever. "Mm mm..." he said, as he squeezed my body against his. He then slid his hands down and squeezed my ass, instantly a stirring sensation between my legs. "Wassup sexy?" I said to him, as I looked at his arms and smooth skin. He looked really good and healthy. He grinned noticing the way I looked at him. "Baby, you brought my clothes?" he asked. "Well dang babe let me get comfortable first, before you start with your clothes." We both laughed. Ra had to make sure everything was right with his clothes and package. "Yes, babe I handled everything," I said smiling. "Ok I have another bag of clothes you have to take home and wash," he said touching his hair.

I laughed at him shaking my head. "What?" he asked, with a smirk on his face. "You are what?" I said grabbing his hands. "Anyways, wassup babe, I miss you like crazy," I said. "Oh yeah? How much do you miss me?" Ra asked laughing. "Stop babe you play too much, but I do miss you," I said, giving him a lush look. He looked at me and gave me a peck on the lips. "I miss you more," he said.

"Babe, why you didn't tell me Kim was pregnant?" Ra asked. I looked puzzled and didn't know what he was talking about. "What are you talking about babe?" I asked, still with a puzzled look on my face. "Yeah, Kim is pregnant! Kareem told me he has a baby on the way," Ra said. I was so pissed. I was furious with Kim. I couldn't believe she didn't tell me she was pregnant. Even though we were not on speaking terms, I still would have supported her, I thought to myself.

"Ra are you serious? I can't believe she didn't tell me she was pregnant. As long as we've been friends, she thinks it's over just like that?" I said to Ra. "Now I'm furious with her." "Calm down Tye. Don't say that because first off, life is too short and it's not that serious. But why are yall fighting anyway?" Ra asked. Ra was so nosy, he knew I didn't like to discuss my friend's business with him. And I never mentioned my man's business to Kim or Tania. It was just a respect thing, to keep friends and relationships separate. I honestly felt it was fake talking about them behind each other's back.

But being that Kim told Kareem, I had to explain to Ra the story. "Babe all I know is, I met her and Tania at Tony Roma's for dinner after I got my hair done. I guess she was upset because I got there 5 minutes late. She started saying some slick shit out of her mouth that I never expected her to ever say, so I checked her. I told her about herself, and we started arguing in the damn restaurant. I haven't spoken to her since. But you know what? Something wasn't right. It's like she was mad about something she thought I said, but who knows." I said explaining everything to Ra.

"Well, whatever it is, yall need to work things out, because yall are best friends and it's stupid. Tye, like I said before, life is too short. You should know that by now," Ra said. As I listened to Ra, I realized he was right and it was stupid. I knew I had to be the bigger person and apologize. Despite my hectic life, I knew I would have to reach out to her. Overall, she was not just a best friend to me, but my sister, who I truly loved.

"Your right babe," I said to him. "Do you speak to Tania?" He asked. "Now Ra, you are too nosy," I said, with my arms folded. We both busted out laughing. Ra was nosy, but I could understand by him being locked up all day, he needed to hear some type of excitement or drama. "Nah for real, because Kareem said he hasn't heard from Toast in a while and he's been acting funny. So that's why I was asking you if you spoke to her." Ra said.

"You know what babe, I haven't heard from Tania since that night Kim and I got into it. She was kind of acting funny, but I didn't pay her any mind. I guess I have to check up on her too," I said. "Let me know," he said. I sucked my teeth. "Boy," I said. "Girl," he said. "Nah for real, because Toast hasn't come up to see me nor answer any of my calls. So, I want to know what is up with him," Ra said, sounding concerned. "Ok, Ra I will find out and check up on it. But in the meantime, you just keep up ya head up and don't worry about the outside life right now."

"I know you have a lot to deal with inside here. That's enough stress in itself, so just stay focused" I said, rubbing his hands. "You know your trial is coming up babe," I said, with a concerned look on my face. "Yeah, I know babe. I'm kind of nervous myself, but things should be good," Ra said.

I could tell Ra was nervous. Who wouldn't be nervous. This was his life and all he had right now. It was indeed a battle we would have to fight together. Whether or not he was found guilty, I was not going to leave him. He was always going to be my man. If I had to spend the rest of my life, loving someone struck in a grey jail cell so be it, I guess. I knew I wasn't leaving him, I was riding out.

"We will beat this," I said, smiling as Ra smiled back. "Yeah I know," he said. "And after all this, we are going to go away. We are going to plan a trip to an island. I will make sure there's a private section for the both of us. We're also going to make love throughout the whole island," he said. I cried as he told me everything he wanted to do, once he got out of there. I loved hearing him talk like that and I couldn't wait until that day came.

"Babe you are so crazy, that's why I love you so much," I said wiping the tears off my face. We spoke about our plans for after he escaped this nightmare, until our visit came to an end. "I hate this part right here," I said. "I know babe, if only I could leave with you," he said. Ra got up with his hands wide open and I slowly got up to hug him. He pulled me close to him. It felt like the first time I fell in love with him. We kissed and of course he squeezed and grabbed my ass. I began to get wet even more. "Umm babe," I said, feeling so profound in the moment.

I looked up into his eyes. A look that meant, I wanted him to do me right there on the table. "See you later," he said, as he gently let go of my waist. He walked to the side, and the tips of my fingers dropped as he walked toward the lineup. "Later Ra," I said softly. My body began to get stiff watching him walk through the double doors. It made my stomach hurt and body cold.

As I got off the bus, I was walking to the parking lot. I saw a young girl holding her baby, as if she was waiting for a ride. I knew visiting hours were over. She looked really familiar to me, but I couldn't remember from where. All I knew was it was too cold for her to be out here waiting, especially with her child; who was crying.

"Hey, do you need help?" I asked her. She looked at me with tears in her eyes. She couldn't even speak. She just cried holding her baby. It suddenly dawned on me who she was. It was the girl who gave me the metro card, when I first came up here to visit Ra.

"Oh my gosh! Hey, are you ok?" I asked, touching her shoulder. She shook her head no and tried to speak. "Don't cry," I said. "Do you need a ride home?" I asked. She nodded her head yes. "Ok I'll take you home," I said to her. We walked to the car, which wasn't too far from the bus stop.

I opened the car door for her, and she slid her son in first, then she got in behind him. I walked to the driver's side and got in. I instantly turned on the heat so she could get a little warmth. My car immediately got warm. "Where do you live?" I asked, as I drove out of the parking lot. "I live in Brooklyn, Clinton Hill," she said, wiping the tears from her face. I knew exactly where that was. Kim lives there, I thought to myself. "I never got your name," I said, looking in the rear-view mirror. "Rena," she said softly. "Ok, my name is Tye. Nice to finally meet you" I said, as we both smiled at each other.

"What is your son's name?" I asked. "Liam..." she said, rocking him on her lap. "Aww so cute," I said. "How old is he?" "He is one, going on two in a couple of days," she said. "Oh yeah that's good," I said smiling at her. "Are you guy's hungry?" I asked. She shook her head no. "I didn't have time to eat because I was rushing up here," she said shaking her head. As she shuddered her head, tears came falling. I didn't know what to say. I knew she was upset and wasn't sure if she wanted to vent, so I drove in silence for a second.

"Well, I could buy you guys something to eat," I said. I was so hungry, I thought to myself. "The only thing in my stomach is toothpaste, that keeps erupting my hunger," I said to her. She slightly laughed. I noticed a Popeye's, so I stopped and ordered an 11-piece chicken with fries and biscuits. I pulled over so I could eat, because I couldn't drive any further on an empty stomach. "Thank you, Tye," she said softly. I winked at her.

I parked the car, we ate and we chatted for a little while. Rena was 20 years old, living with her grandmother. She was beautiful and had a nice shape. She was very respectful and sweet also. Her baby father was locked up for a gun charge and drugs. Rena had explained how she went to visit, and couldn't see her boyfriend because another girl was on the visit. That's why she was upset, and I understood why.

I finally reached Clinton Hill. It was so crazy how Rena lived in the same building as Kim, but on a different floor. I thought about visiting Kim, but I didn't want to show up unannounced. "Thank you so much Tye.! I appreciate this, you were such a big help" Rena said. "Girl I told you one day I would return the favor. You never know how or when good deeds will come back. You're Welcome." I said with a smile.

We exchanged numbers, and I told her I would keep in touch with her. I looked at Rena as family. Another little sister of mine, I thought to myself.

"Call me whenever or when you make your next visit," I said to her. She rolled her eyes, saying she would not visit again and it was over. "Good choice," I said to her. She closed the door with one hand and had her son on the other side. I watched her walk towards the building, making sure she got in safe. I almost decided to see Kim, but I didn't want to intrude, because I didn't know how she was feeling. So, I just decided to go home.

Before I knew it, I was home. I prepared a nice bath and had my phone ready just in case Ra called. I eased myself into the tub and relaxed. As my body soaked, the hot water felt so good against my back. Even though, from time to time I would get a sharp pain, I was relaxed for the moment, and it eased my pain.

As I thought about that night, it amazed me, how I could have been paralyzed. Look how God pulled me through. I am so thankful to be here and walking. Tears poured down my face, because no one could understand the joy I felt, when I said the Lord's names. He can do miracles and get you through anything. A few moments later, my phone rang. And there you had it, it was Ra calling. Ummm, I thought to myself. "Hey, sexy…," already his voice had me melting…

CHAPTER 17

It's now June, and Ra is still locked up. His trial hasn't started yet, but it will in a couple of days. Mr. Bennett has prolonged his case for a while, just to gain time to gather more evidence. Mr. Bennett had been working hard on Ra's case. He dug up facts to prove his innocence, that he wouldn't reveal to me. All Mr. Bennett would say every time I asked about the situation, was that everything would to be ok. At times I would get mad at him, wanting to curse him out. Then I figured he knew best. Mr. Bennett did warn me that something fishy was going to happen during the trial. I became very nervous and concerned, because I didn't know what to expect.

I honestly was afraid to find out what was going to take place. It still had been days since I'd eaten or slept. As Ra's trial days began to get closer, my habits started to get worse. My prayers helped to comfort me, along with Ra's help at times. Being in the house made me sick to my stomach, and I worried about unnecessary things. So, I made it my business to get out. I still hadn't patched up things with Kim yet, so I decided I should be the one to reconcile. I reached out to Kim to meet me for lunch and she agreed to do so. I was excited she agreed.

I was meeting Kim at a restaurant called Pio, in Mid-Manhattan. The food was so delicious and it was beautiful inside. Ra and I used to go there all the time during lunch hours. I made it my business to arrive early, since she fusses about me being late all the time. As I sat and waited, I thought about how she would react. How would she act towards me since we had the argument? It had been months since I'd heard from or seen her. At this point, I didn't know how she felt about our friendship anymore.

Within a few minutes, I received a text message from Kim saying she was here. Wow, she did show up, I thought to myself. I knew how Kim could be at times. I got out of the car and walked across the street towards her. Good thing I had a close parking spot. To my surprise, Kim's belly bump was showing. I covered my mouth with my hands as I got closer to her. She looked at me and smiled. She then put her hands over her mouth as tears rolled down. Kim was excited to see me as well.

I reached out with my arms and embraced her with nothing but love. I hugged Kim tight, and she hugged me back. As we hugged each other, rocking back and forth, we both apologized. "I'm sorry," she said softly, and I said it back while tears poured down. We let go of one another and wiped the tears that fell from our eyes. "Aww," I said, as I rubbed her stomach. "I'm an auntie..." "Yup and you will make a good auntie." We both laughed. "I'm hungry," Kim said. "Yeah girl, you're eating for two now," I said laughing. Within moments the waiter came out saying our table was ready. "Perfect timing," Kim said, and we both entered the restaurant.

Kim and I chatted for a while. We spoke about old times and her new bundle of joy. Kim and Kareem were so happy about having a baby. I was so excited as well, as if it were me. "Kim, I want to apologize to you. Whatever I did I'm sorry" I said, taking a sip of my drink. "I could have waited to get my hair done, but girl I needed something to make me feel better," I said laughing. "No Tye, I'm sorry I even listened to Tania," Kim said as she was chewing her food. I didn't know what she meant by that though. "What do you mean Tania?" I asked, with a confused look on my face.

Kim chewed the remaining food in her mouth and took a sip of water. "This chick Tania!, said you told her my engagement wouldn't last, and you were talking about my relationship to her," Kim said. As Kim told me all the things Tania said, I was looking at Kim like she was crazy. It wasn't that I didn't believe Kim, it was just shocking what she told me. I never would have thought Tania would say anything like that.

My mouth was wide open as Kim told me all of the lies and things Tania was saying. "Kim," I said, but before I could even say what I wanted, Kim said she knew it wasn't true. "I had realized it after the fact, once I noticed her not saying anything. But Tye you don't understand, these hormones had me going crazy at the time. I couldn't control my anger," Kim said. I understood what she was saying, because I was once pregnant before. But I was still thrown off about Tania. Why would she do something like this? I thought to myself.

"Kim let me ask you a question," I said. Kim looked at me while chewing her food. "Have you heard from Tania since the day of argument?" I asked her. Kim thought about it and said, "No I haven't. I haven't even tried reaching out to her since. Once I got home, I was so upset that I told Kareem about what happened. He told me that you took him to pick out the ring. He also told me that you suggested he propose the night of Ra's birthday celebration. I was too ashamed to call and apologize, because I felt dumb. Kareem also told me that he hasn't heard from Toast since Ra's birthday, and that he was acting funny towards him. So, I felt like a bitch," Kim said shaking her head.

"Wow! Kim, I can't believe this. But you know what, I'm not trying to reach out to her anymore. I will leave it alone and let God handle it. The way I've been feeling lately, I could fight Tania, but girl I'm not going there." "Tye! Just know Kareem, Kyra and I are here for you," Kim said. "Kyra?" I started smiling. "We are having a girl,"

Kim said. "A Girl?" I said repeating what Kim said. I was too excited. "We are actually having a girl," Kim expressed, also repeating herself.

"Now you know Kareem is going to be overprotective," Kim said, shaking her head. As Kim spoke, I couldn't help but smile. I was truly happy for the both of them. "Kim I'm so happy for you guys. I really am," I said to Kim. "Thanks, girl," Kim said, and we kept the conversation going.

That evening we spoke about everything. Kim wanted me to plan her baby shower as well. I couldn't have been more excited to plan my niece's shower. She also told me that I would be the godmother of her child, and Ra the godfather. I was even happier. Kim had made my day. I was happy that we were able to work out our differences and become friends again. I felt much better about myself. Kim and I wound up having a good date and planned to do it more often. "I love you," I said to Kim "And I love you more sis." We then continued to gossip about Kyra.

Ra...

As he looked out of the small box window, he couldn't wait to be free. Six months felt like his whole life, and Ra was ready to go. He had one more day before his trial was to start. Ra was anxious and nervous at the same time. He just wanted to wake up next to Tye and forget the trial. Ra didn't want to see or hear what was going to take place, but he knew he still had to deal with it.

Ra thought about what would happen, and what would be the outcome constantly. He didn't want too think so much about it, because he knew it would drive him crazy. As Ra looked out the window, he said a prayer out loud and didn't care if anyone thought he was talking himself.

"Dear Lord,

I've been locked up for six months and may not understand why I was in this predicament, but I know things happen for reasons. I have been reading scriptures and saying prayers, because I realize I have no one to turn to besides you. The dream I dreamt of, I know it was a sign from you. I thank you for showing me the truth. I couldn't tell anyone what you have revealed to me but I do know you are here for me. I know I can't make it in this world without you. Even though I believed in you, I still never made time to pray to you. To keep my faith and live for you. I don't know anyone who understands me more than you. The position I'm in right now has me sick to my stomach. I can't even remember that night, and will probably never remember that night. But I do pray that you forgive me for my sins. If I took that a life, Lord forgive me. It was not my intentions to kill anyone, only to protect myself. I know I have made a few bad choices in life and never asked forgiveness. I stand here now to ask for forgiveness, and to wash my sins away. Forgive me for the ones I know of and the ones I don't know of. I have positive thoughts for my trial. I do believe that I will win, even though it's not about winning, but about the truth. Maybe I had to open up my eyes to understand why this took place. I know things don't happen for no reason, so there's a reason behind it. Everything you do is for a purpose. I do pray that I am humble and I get justice in the end. Lord, I pray for a second chance at life. A chance to better myself through you. I will be a changed and better person. I ask for changes in my life as well as a new beginning. Thank you. AMEN!"

After Ra said his prayers, he realized he wound up on his knees. He felt relief from what he was going through inside. Ra knew he had to be more into the Lord. Not just because of the situation he was dealing with, but because he wanted to do better and do right.

"Yo!" When Ra looked up to see who was speaking to him, he noticed Reggie near his cell. Ra lifted up from his knees and walked towards Reggie. "You good bro?" Reggie asked dropping his head. "Yeah I'm good," Ra said with a smirk. "Good, I requested off to be there at your trial date," Reggie said. Ra grinned. "Really man? Yo, I appreciate it." Ra said. "You know we brothers," Reggie said. Reggie didn't have to take off, but he and Ra were family. Reggie didn't care if he wasn't supposed to be there, because he was going anyway.

"Well I'll see you later," Reggie said, as he walked out of Ra's cell. Ra stood there, then turned back around to the little window he found himself praying to.

CHAPTER 18

Tye…

Early morning with the sun shining brightly through my window. It looked like a beautiful day. Today was the start of Ra's trial, and I was nervous. I had to use the bathroom three times before I left the house, and my stomach hurt like crazy. I didn't have an appetite and honestly, I wasn't feeling well. My nerves were acting up, and I began to have sweats. I really didn't want to tell anyone how I was feeling. So when Kim had texted me to ask how I was doing, I pretended everything was ok.

Kareem and Kim were going to meet me at the court. I knew the trial started at 9 am, but I didn't know how long it would be. I heard it could take up to four months. But Mr. Bennett said he was only going to give it a few days or so, because he had his evidence. I guess I'd have to see how the trial played out. After my fourth time using the bathroom, I rushed to shower. I straightened my hair and put on my yellow, blazer pants suit, with my Jimmy Choo, black and white pumps.

I then gave Diamond some fresh food and water and headed to the door. For some reason, I procrastinated this morning, but I still made it out on time. Getting to the courts was a task. The Brooklyn Bridge was so jammed up, I was glad I'd left the house earlier than I planned. After the traffic jam on the bridge, I still arrived early.

I parked my car in the parking lot that was near Supreme Family Courthouse on Jay street. I arrived early and walked across the street for some Starbucks.

I needed some coffee to calm my nerves, and hopefully, I'd be back to myself. Waiting on line for my coffee, I spotted Mr. Bennett sitting down reviewing some papers and drinking coffee. "Good morning, Mr. Bennett," I said, walking up to him. "Good morning Tye!" he said, putting his hands out so I could sit down. I pulled the seat from under the table and sat down. "How are you this morning?" he asked, looking at his notes. "I'm ok," I said, taking a sip of my coffee. "Good! That's what I like to hear." I smiled softly.

"Don't worry everything is taken care of?" Mr. Bennett said. He packed up his papers and said, "Let the fiasco begin." He took his cup of coffee and put it in the air, walking out the door. I looked speechless because I didn't know what to say. But if he said everything would be ok, I'm guessing it was going to be ok, I thought to myself, as I drunk my coffee. "Let the fiasco begin," I repeated leaving out of Starbucks.

As I got off the elevator, I saw a lot of people outside the courtroom. Some looked familiar, while others didn't. There must have been a lot of commotion, because alot of court officers stood outside. I didn't bother to see what happened, I just walked inside the courtroom. Looking at the crowd of people inside, I didn't know if there were any more seats available. Chills instantly ran down my spine. I noticed Kim and Kareem sitting next to others.

"Hey guys," I said softly, as I walked towards Kareem and Kim. Kareem got up, gave me a hug and kissed me on the cheek, then let me through to sit down. Kim then gave me a hug before I sat down. "Girl who are all these people?" I whispered to Kim. "Girl those are Kareem and Ra's friends and some other dudes." My mouth fell wide open. Within seconds, the crowd of people that were outside came inside the courtroom.

A group of people came on our side, and the others parted to the other side. There were two officers at each side. The courtroom was packed, and I still couldn't believe Ra had so many supporters. As I turned to look around, I spotted Reggie in the corner. He winked at me, and I smiled at him. I felt so relieved that my nerves calmed down. "All arise!" the officer said. We all stood up, and Kim struggled to get up. Kareem helped her up. I wanted to laugh hard, but I held it in.

Mr. Bennett walked through with another guy behind him. As Mr. Bennett stood up, he turned and looked at me and turned back around. Judge Kovac was a judge that did not give any justice. I heard in every murder case, he would sentence them to 35 or more years to life. The judge was a jerk, and I couldn't wait until this trial was over.

As Judge Kovac walked out, he had a disturbed look on his face, and I could tell he was going to be a problem. I just kept my faith strong because only God has the last say so.

Once he sat down, everyone sat down as well. "The Case ending in 13-cv-6715, People vs. Rasheem Mills. Court is in session," the judge said, as he slammed his gavel. "Banging! Let's goo…"

CHAPTER 19

Ra came walking out with his hands cuffed behind his back. I noticed his facial expression, observing the groups of people in the courtroom. His eyes widened with surprise by the crowd. Ra slightly grinned once he saw my smile. I melted inside, yet still feeling nervous at the same time. Mr. Bennett sat right next to Ra and whispered something in his ear. Ra nodded his head and sat straight up. It was the DA's opportunity to present their case. The DA was Don Smith, a Korean Lawyer, who had won many murder cases. He was well known to be a good DA and had never lost a case. I researched Don Smith and had found he was brilliant.

"Good Morning Jurors," Mr. Smith said, as he got up from his seat. As he paced back and forth, from left to right, he spoke to the jurors. I examined the jurors and noticed how their facial expressions looked. Some looked as if they didn't care, but most looked interested to know the facts. There sat 3 Whites, 2 Spanish, 1 Mexican, 4 Blacks and 2 Asians. Most of them looked young, but a few looked older.

Mr. Smith began his presentation while maintaining eye contact with the jurors. "I'm here today to state the facts of a murder. A murderer sits is in the room today, for killing an innocent man. That man right there has killed Famedon Young. He is a murderer!" Mr. Smith said pointing at Ra. As Mr. Smith, pointed his finger towards Ra, I got mad. Tears welled up in my eyes, and I just wanted to scream. I held back the tears and looked at Kim, then back towards the DA. I hated to sit and hear the things he called Ra.

"I'm here today to send this man to jail for life. I will tell you everything you need to know about what took place on January 1, 2013, and who is Famed Young. I have a witness today who will testify against Rasheem Mills. My witness will tell you what he saw Rasheem Mills do the day of January First" I looked confused, and looked at Kim. Kim, Kareem and I, all looked at each other with confused looks on our faces. I shrugged my shoulders at Kareem and Kim not knowing what was about to go down. I began to get sick to the stomach.

I noticed Ra whisper something in Mr. Bennett's ear, and Mr. Bennett nodded his head. The room was silent for a moment. I saw the DA still pacing back and forth and pointing fingers at Ra. I was fading in and out, daydreaming of how I was actually going through this. I couldn't hold back the tears, and they poured down my face as everyone sat still. I felt a hand rub my back, and the soft touch of a hand being gently placed on mine. I immediately knew God was calming me down.

"Your honor, I have my witness," Mr. Smith said, looking up at the judge. The judge told the court officer to bring his witness into the room. As the officer walked back into the courtroom, I was in owe. My mouth widened from shock. I couldn't believe what I saw. Kim looked at me, and I looked at her. We had stupid looks on our faces. We were in complete disbelief. Kareem blurted out, "Fag!" and the officer told him to be quiet. Kim grabbed Kareem's hand to calm him down, and he just had a pissed look on his face.

"I call Eli Grant to the stand," the DA said. As Eli walked towards the stand, I grilled him so hard, I know he felt me staring. I couldn't believe Toast was doing this to Ra, after everything Ra had done for Toast. There had been times when Ra had bailed Toast out of jail for DWI and even helped him out, when he was facing a murder charge last year. I looked to my left to see if I saw Tania over there, but I didn't see her.

Then I glanced back over and saw her in the corner. She looked at me and turned her head quickly. I just shook my head. Toast stood up with his right hand raised up and his left hand on the bible. "Repeat after me," the court officer said. "I solemnly swear to tell the truth the whole truth and nothing but the truth so help me God." "I do," Toast said. I shook my head. "Already he is lying," Kim said. Toast sat down with his hands folded. I kept staring at him hard. He knew we were staring at him, but he never looked our way.

Ra remained calm, and I wondered if Ra knew Toast was testifying against him. I knew Ra knew this the whole time, and didn't want to say anything, I thought to myself.

"Mr. Grant, please tell the court about New Year's Day," Mr. Smith said to Toast.

Toast took a sip of water and cleared his throat. "I was celebrating a birthday for a friend." "Which friend was it? Please state the name," Mr. Smith said. "Rasheem Mills," Toast said. "Can you please point, so the jury knows who Rasheem is?" Mr. Smith said. Toast raised up his hand, pointing his finger towards Rasheem. He couldn't even look at Ra. "Ok tell us what happened," Mr. Smith said.

"We were celebrating Rasheem's birthday, along with other friends." "Where was the party located?" Mr. Smith asked. "In Brooklyn at Dumbo Lounge," Toast stated. "Were you and Rasheem drinking?" Mr. Smith asked. "Yes, I had a few drinks." "How many drinks?" asked Mr. Smith. "I would say about 2 drinks." I looked at Toast shaking my head. Not only because he was lying but because he knew damn well, he didn't have just two drinks. He should have said two bottles. I thought to myself.

"So, can you remember what took place that night?" Mr. Smith asked. "Yes," Toast stated. "Please finish telling the jurors what took place," Mr. Smith said, standing behind the podium. "Towards the end of the night, we were getting ready to leave. So, I started walking towards the front, and I didn't see Rasheem near me. When I turned around, I saw him arguing.

I rushed back over there because, I didn't know what was going on. So, when I reached Rasheem, I noticed he was arguing with my cousin." "Please tell the Jurors who your cousin is" Mr. Smith said. "Famedon Young." "Please continue," Mr. Smith said. "I grabbed Rasheem back and tried to break up the fight, but he wouldn't listen to me." "Did you state to Rasheem that he was your cousin?" Mr. Smith asked. "Rasheem knew that was my cousin, he knows my family," Toast said.

I turned to look at Kim, and she rolled her eyes. I couldn't even say anything after that. "Please continue," Mr. Smith said, "Rasheem ignored what I was saying, and out of nowhere, I saw Rasheem shoot my cousin" Toast paused for a second and was silent. He held down his head and put his fingers towards his eyes.

"Un-fucking believable," I said. Was he sitting there crying? I know this has to be a joke, I said to myself. I began to get mad, but I had to hold my composure. Toast wiped the fake tears from his face and held his head back up. "Where did he shoot Famedon Young?" Mr. Smith said. "He shot him in the chest and then in the stomach," Toast stated.

"Why when the police arrived, you weren't there?" Mr. Smith asked. "The reason I wasn't there was because, I was scared when Famedon got shot. I didn't want to be implicated, and I couldn't explain to my family that Famedon was killed," Toast said. "Have you spoken to Rasheem since this situation?" Mr. Smith asked. "No, I haven't heard from or seen him since that night." "And why is that?" Mr. Smith asked. "Because he killed my cousin!" Toast said, as he looked at Ra. "No further questions your honor."

It was Mr. Bennett's turn to ask Toast questions about that night, during cross-examination. "Good Morning Eli, or should I say Toast?" "Toast is what Rasheem and his friends call you right?" "Yes, Toast is the name they call me," Toast stated. "Why does Rasheem call you Toast?" Mr. Bennett asked. "Because I'm always celebrating," Toast said. "How long have you known Rasheem?" Mr. Bennett asked. "A long time" Toast stated. "Please give a specific time," Mr. Bennett stated, while standing at the podium. "For 8 years I had known Rasheem," Toast said. "For eight years you've known Rasheem, and you stated that he killed your cousin?" Mr. Bennett said with his eyebrow raised up. "Yes sir," Toast said looking down. "If you and Rasheem were friends for eight years, why would he kill someone whom you were related to you?" Mr. Bennett asked, pacing back and forth.

Toast shrugged his shoulder. "You must answer so we can hear you" the judge stated. "I don't know," Toast said. "What did Rasheem kill your cousin with?" "A gun," Toast said, but in a sarcastic way. "So, you actually saw Mr. Mills pull out his gun and shoot Famedon?" Mr. Bennett asked. "Yes, I saw Rasheem pull out his gun and start shooting at my cousin," Toast said, sounding agitated.

"Can you please demonstrate to the jury how Rasheem shot your cousin. With what hand, and from what position did he shoot your cousin?" Mr. Bennett asked. "I object!" Mr. Smith intercede. I will allow it the judge said. Toast couldn't demonstrate, he just sat in complete shock and stared without saying a word. "We're waiting," Mr. Bennett said. Toast didn't move, nor attempt to say anything. "You must give a demonstration the judge had stated, with his hands under his chin. "I can't recall," Toast stated, looking at Mr. Bennett. "So how do you know that Mr. Mills killed your cousin with a gun?"

"You just stated he pulled out the gun and started shooting."

Toast paused for a second and held his head down. He started shaking his head, as tears fell down his eyes. "I object!" Mr. Smith said. "Overruled," the judge stated. Toast didn't answer the question. "No further questions," Mr. Bennett said, walking back to his seat.

"You may step down," the judge said to Toast. Toast lifted up his head and stepped down off of the podium. He stepped down and winked at Ra, with a devilish grin on his face. He then walked over to where Kim, Kareem and I sat and winked his eye. I just wanted to slap him, but I held my composure.

I was so upset, but I didn't let him see my facial expression. I grinned back letting him know I wasn't fazed by him. "It's now 12:30pm. I'm going to recess for lunch, and I expect everybody back at 1:30pm." the judge stated. The court officer put handcuffs on Ra, as he tried to sneak a peek at me. I saw him glance from the side of his head, and smile. I smiled back even though he couldn't see me.

The court officers had to exit the jurors, and we had to wait until they were all the way downstairs. Being that the courtroom was packed, I waited until they were cleared out first, so that I could at least speak to Mr. Bennett. I couldn't wait until I talked to Mr. Bennett. I couldn't believe what I'd just witnessed and had so many questions to ask Mr. Bennett.

Once the courtroom cleared, I noticed Mr. Bennett packing up his papers into his briefcase. He walked through the double doors and looked at me. I followed behind him. "What is going on?" I asked Mr. Bennett, as soon as we reached outside the courtroom. He pulled me over to the side near a corner, and placed his briefcase on the ground.

"Did you see how scared he was? Did you notice that he couldn't answer any of my questions?" As Mr. Bennett was talking I just dazed out. I didn't think whatever he was saying was funny. I honestly thought it wasn't funny at all. I just had a blank look on my face and stared at Mr. Bennett as he spoke.

"He will be ok Tye, I promise you that," Mr. Bennett said, touching both of my shoulders. I slightly smiled and watched him pick up his briefcase and walk past me. I slowly walked past Kim and Kareem and noticed Reggie sitting down. I walked into the bathroom. Before I could even close the bathroom door, Kim was right behind me. I just slumped in her arms, while my face hit the top of her belly bump and cried. I cried so hard I started snorting.

Kim rocked me and touched the side of my face, telling me to calm my nerves. I calmed my nerves, but the tears just kept running down my face, pouring onto her stomach. But Kim didn't pay it any mind, she just rocked me until my tears started to dry up and I calmed down. "You better?" Kim asked. I nodded my head yes and slowly lifted from her.

"Kim this shit got me crazy. I don't know what to think anymore. My nerves are shot, and my stomach hurts like crazy. I'm trying to be cool, but this is hard," I said to Kim. "I know what you mean Tye. But what I can tell you is, you have to let God handle it. God has the final word, not Toast, the jurors or that fat ass judge. Not even Mr. Bennett, just God. I know you're nervous and you're thinking the worst right now. But erase all the negative thoughts in your head, and let God do his work.

All we can do is support Ra," Kim said. Everything she said was right, and it made me feel better. "Thank you," I said with a shaky voice. It sounded like I was going to cry, but I held it in. I hugged her and I smiled. "Thanks, Kim," I said softly. "You're welcome, now let's get something to eat because I'm starving." I shook my head. "Greedy Kim and Kyra," I said as, we walked out of the bathroom.

CHAPTER 20

"All arise!" the Judge wobbled back to his seat, followed by the jurors. Once we arrived, Ra was already sitting down, so I couldn't see his face this time. "I hope everyone enjoyed their lunch, now let's continue where we left off." "Thank you, your honor," Mr. Smith said, as he got up from his seat, buttoning up his tight blazer. He then walked over to the jurors. "I hope you understand what my witness saw the night of Famedon Young's murder. He was tremendously scared, hurt and afraid. He was in a state of shock because his cousin had been killed, right in front of him, by his so-called best friend. He was scared to be the person to tell his beloved family that his cousin had been killed. If you heard well and listened to his testimony, I hope you make the right decision to send this murderer to jail for the rest of his life."

"He has killed an innocent man for no reason. Famedon had 2 kids, a girlfriend and family that's been left behind from a senseless murder. Please send Rasheem Mills to jail for the killing of Famedon Young. Thank you, jurors." Mr. Smith said as he walked over to his seat smirking at Mr. Bennett.

It was now Mr. Bennett's turn to give his argument for Rasheem. Even though Kim gave me the right encouragement, I was still nervous. I rubbed my hands together, squeezing tightly, and Kim touched my hand. I looked at her, and she gave me that look like, remember what I told you, and I calmed down. Mr. Bennett got to the stand. He looked at the crowd, then looked at Rasheem. I was so confused as to why he did that, but I just waited for him to speak.

"Good afternoon Jurors!" Mr. Bennett said. They just looked at him. Some smiled, while others just sat there with a straight face. Today, I'm here on behalf of Rasheem Mills, the victim. Who is here today, because he was falsely accused of the murder of Famedon Young. I have a witness that saw everything that night. Unlike Mr. Smith's witness, mine is uncapable of fabricating a story, as to what took place that night. Once you see the events from this point of view, I'm confident you will find my client, NOT GUILTY!". Mr. Bennett said with a smile. He had such confidence about him, like he just took pride in what he believed in. I was thankful he was giving his all to help Ra out.

As the screen came down and the lights went out, I became confused as to what was going to take place. I looked at Kim and Kareem, and they looked back at me, with concerned looks on their faces. Then I realized it was a video that Mr. Bennett was showing. Everybody in the courtroom made a sound, and the court officer had to shut them up. My heart beat faster and faster, and I was dying to know what took place that night.

What showed in the footage of the video, was when Ra and I first entered the lounge. We then saw Kareem, Kim, Toast, and Tania. It showed us walking from the front to the back of the lounge. Everything was set up as nicely as I had imagined and the crowd wasn't so bad. It then skipped to the part where Kareem proposed to Kim and when the ball dropped. It showed the dispute between Tania and Toast arguing, and him putting his hands all up in her face. He was so aggressive.

As I sat and watched I smiled, because I kind of remembered this part of the night. How the party mixers were exposed everywhere, and everybody was with his or her loved ones. I looked at Kim, and she smiled at me. Then it skipped to another part. This is where the drama began. A crowd came in of Famedon and his peoples. We saw Ra say something to us, and we all got up and started walking through. I guess at this point we all were leaving.

I saw Tania and Kim walking through, and got separated from Toast and Kareem. I was still next to Ra. When I saw Kim walking, I started to follow Kim, but was grabbed by a guy. He kept pulling and touching me, and I was telling him to stop. The guy who was pulling me was Famedon. My mouth widened, and I was in shock. First, because I really didn't remember that, and second was because wow, out of all people who grabbed, me it had to be Famedon.

It showed Ra looking around as if he was looking for someone. It then showed how Fame was standing behind Ra once he turned back around. That's when the drama happened. Ra bumped into Fame face to face and Fame jumped at Ra. It showed how Fame was yelling and being really aggressive towards Ra, putting his hands in Ra's face. Ra was just standing there saying something, as if he was trying to defend himself. It also showed that Famedon was holding something, but we couldn't quite see what it was. Now Ra was arguing back at Fame. Suddenly Fame's friends came surrounding Ra. It looked like they were going to jump him.

Ra tried walking away, but one of Fame's friends grabbed his arm. Both of them were now in Ra's face. Toast came through and jumped in the guy's face, and they started arguing. It also showed a bottle in Toast's hand, as if he was going to hit the guy in the face with the bottle. Kareem then walks over to Fame and says something. Fame ignored what Kareem said and pushed him out the way.

Fame then grabbed what was in his pocket and hit Ra in the face. It was a gun that Fame had in his pocket the whole time. Ra stumbled as if he was going to hit the floor, but held his balance. He came back at Fame, and they started fighting. As they were fighting, the crowd made a delayed disappearing act. It showed me laying down on the floor and Kim covering her mouth crying. A guy then lifted me up and walked me out with Kim behind us.

It also showed what took place with the police. I couldn't even watch anymore. Tears welled up in my eyes, because I couldn't believe this took place at the beginning of the New Year. Maybe this whole time I thought to myself that Ra did it, but he really didn't murder anyone. The details that took place in the tape showed alot. I was shocked, not because I couldn't remember, but because who would have ever known a camera was recording the whole time.

The video took up half the court session and then we recessed until tomorrow morning. I also knew that I had to go up on the stand and testify about the shooting in my lower back. I really wasn't ready to answer any questions.

I arrived home baffled about what took place in the video. It really showed that Famedon started the whole thing. I was so confused. If that was Toast's cousin, why didn't he say anything or try to prevent the situation from happening? Toast provoked most of the fight. I can't believe Tania couldn't even speak to me. She forgot how once before she had to deal with a situation like this, when Toast was facing a murder charge. I had been there with her the whole time to back her up.

I thought about the millions of people that were in the line of fire. Not one was hurt but me. Things just happen in mysterious ways. I took a nice shower and eased my way into bed. Diamond jumped on my bed, sensing something wasn't right with me. I patted the bed so she can walk towards me. She slowly walked over with thousands of kisses. "You know today will be the last day you sleep with me, because you know Ra hates you in the bed," I said to her, pointing my finger. She licked it, and I picked her up and held her tight. "He will be home tomorrow Diamond, I promise that," I said, as she and I slowly drifted off into sleep.

CHAPTER 21

Day 2

"All rise!", the court officer said, as the judge walked in and sat down. Once again, he announced his morning speech to the jurors, and again I became deaf to his words. I was so nervous, because I had to get up on the stand to testify about that night. "I would like to call my next witness to the stand," Mr. Bennett said. I was in such a daze, I didn't hear much but, Tye Rene.

I suddenly snapped out of my daze and cleared my mind. I slowly got up, as Kim held my hand and quickly let go. I looked from Kareem to Reggie, who sat next to each other. At this point, the whole courtroom stared at me. I noticed from the side of my eye, that Toast and Tania also stared at me. I glanced back at them, and Tania held her head down, trying not to make eye contact. Bitch! I said to myself and continue to walk to the stand.

It felt like forever when I started to walk to the stand. My body was dragging, and I began to get stiff. For some strange reason, my back started to hurt again. The court officer helped me up, and I sat down. Wow, I thought to myself. There was a full house. The courtroom was packed, and again I became so nervous. "Please place your left hand on the bible and raise your right hand. Please repeat after me," the officer said. "Do you swear to tell the truth, the whole truth and nothing but the truth, so help you God." I repeated the words and said, "I do." "Please be seated," he said. I swiped my dress underneath me and slowly sat down.

As I looked up, I saw Ra looking at me. I could see his facial expression and that grin on his face. I wanted to laugh so hard, but I held it in. I knew what that face meant. I slightly smirked and blushed a little. Ra then winked at me, and I melted inside.

"Good morning Ms. Rene," Mr. Bennett said.

"Good morning," I said softly, speaking into the microphone. "To my understanding, you and Rasheem are a couple?" Mr. Bennett asked. "Yes," I said. "How long have you been in a relationship with Rasheem?" "Four years we've been together," I said with a smile. "Has he ever done anything to hurt you, since you've been in a relationship with him?" Mr. Bennett asked. "No, never," I said.

"The night of New Year's Eve, you gave him a party correct?" "Yes," I said.

"So, you coordinated the guest list, and everything?" Mr. Bennett asked. "Yes, I did," I said.

"Who did you invite to Rasheem's party?" Mr. Bennett asked.

"I invited close friends, family, and friends of Rasheem, whom he worked with, "I said, taking a deep breath. "Did you know who Famedon Young was?" Mr. Bennett asked. "No, I didn't," I stated.

"Did you know he was related to Toast?" "No, I didn't," I stated.

"Did you invite Famedon that night?" Mr. Bennett asked. "No, I did not invite him."

"So only whoever was on the guest list was invited?"

"Correct," I stated.

I became so calm, because they were simple questions being asked. Even though I wasn't aware of the questions, they were pretty simple. "Do you remember what took place that night with the shooting?" Mr. Bennett asked. That was when it really hit me.

I began to tear up, and tension overwhelmed my body. "No." I said, and paused for a moment to gather my thoughts. "I can't remember what took place that night. All I know is that I woke up in a hospital bed, being told I was almost paralyzed." By this time, tears were already running down my face.

The court officer came over and brought me a tissue, and I wiped the tears from my face. I wouldn't dare look at Ra, because I knew he felt bad. So, I kept my attention elsewhere. "And where were you shot?" Mr. Bennett asked. "I was shot in the lower back, near my spine," I said dryly, as tears continued to fall. I heard a lot of people whispering, but I blocked it out and ignored them. After several more questions, Mr. Bennett paused and stared at the jury.

"How long did it take you to recover from your injuries?" Mr. Bennett asked. "It took me almost a month to be release from the hospital, but I'm still suffering from pain,' I said. At this time my tears kept pouring down my face. I couldn't stop the crying. "I know this is hard for you," Mr. Bennett said. There was a silence in the court room and all you heard was me weeping.

I gathered myself together and dried my tears. My nerves were settling and more questions were asked.

"Thank you, Ms. Rene," Mr. Bennett said, and walked back over to Ra. I thought it was over for the questioning, but Mr. Smith had to cross-examine me. Oh gosh, I thought to myself.

"Ms. Rene," Mr. Smith said, walking towards me with his tight blazer. I know this is a difficult time, especially having to deal with your boyfriend shooting you. 'What!" I said out loud. I'd had enough of Mr. Smith and his smart comments.

"Is it true that Rasheem has put his hands on you in the past?" My eyes squinted, and I wanted to come across the stand and smack him. I couldn't allow him to get the best of me though. "Rasheem has never put his hands on me, "I stated.

"So, he never threw you out of the house, or slapped you before? Never?" Mr. Smith asked. "OBJECTION!" Mr. Bennett said "Overruled," the judge said. "Did he tell you to hold his gun that night?" Mr. Smith asked. "He didn't have a gun," I said with an attitude. I was getting annoyed, but I couldn't allow him to see my emotions.

I had a smirk on my face the whole time Mr. Smith came at me with all of his accusations. I knew Tania and Toast had something to do with it, because there were questions he was asking about Tania. Everything was overruled, every time Mr. Bennett said "objection." He damn near had me up on the stand for 10 minutes, and only one question was answered.

"Thank you for your time, you may step down," the judge said. "You're welcome," I said with a smirk, and walked down from the stand. When I walked over to my seat, Tania looked at me, and she just stared. She didn't even blink her eyes, she just stared. I guess that was a way of her saying she was sorry, but I didn't care about her apology.

Now that both parties had stated their facts and presented their evidence, the jurors had to deliberate. I was confused because I thought we had a couple of days to this trial.

My heart was pounding. This was the day that would determine if Ra was coming home or not. Scared couldn't describe how I was feeling. Every emotion you could possibly think of happened to me. In the meantime, "You can go out to lunch and be back at 1:30pm. Hopefully, the jurors will have came to a verdict," the judge said.

Once the jurors left the courtroom, I noticed Mr. Bennett talking to Ra in his ear. He shook his hand, and Ra embraced him back with a side hug. When the jurors cleared the court, the officer came over to clear the rest of the courtroom. Groups of people got up and walked out. Again Kim, Kareem, Reggie and I waited until they were entirely out of the way. Ra was still sitting down, and I was hoping he would turn around, so I could look at him. But the court officer wouldn't move out of the way.

"Let's go!" Kareem said. We all got up and headed outside the courtroom. "I don't think I could eat yall. I'm going to stay right here." "Girl if you don't put something in your stomach," Kim said. "I know, I'm just to nervous, you know." "We are all are nervous Tye!" "Yeah I don't think I can eat either," Reggie said. "Nah I can't either," Kareem said. Kim stood there with her hands on her hip. "You see, I can't mess with yall." We all busted out laughing. "You guys know I'm pregnant and I'm starving." Kim sat on the bench, pulled out a sandwich from her bag and started eating. I thought I was going to pee my pants. "Nobody but you Kim," I said, laughing so hard. Reggie walked away smiling, while Kareem just looked at her.

"At least you made me feel better," I said to her. She nodded her head and continued to eat her sandwich. We stayed outside in the waiting area, and talked about everything. Kareem and Reggie had brought up memories about Ra, and actually became good friends as well. We did have good memories of Toast and Tania, but we were so shocked that they did something like this.

We weren't going to try and figure it out, so we just had to accept everything for what it really was. "When Ra comes home today, we are going on a trip together, because I know he will need it." "Yeah, I sure know I need it," Kareem said looking at Kim. "What you looking at me like that for?" Kim said drinking water. "Yes, we can sure use a trip together," Reggie said. We were having a good conversation, and already the court session was about to reconvene. We noticed the crowd of people were coming back. It was now 2:00pm and the jurors still hadn't reached a verdict yet. I then began to get nervous. "What's taking so long?" I asked to Kim. "Girl they are only 30 minutes late." I laughed, but I was dead serious. It felt like forever.

Within moments of me complaining, the court officer told us we could go back in. There were a lot of cops outside the courtroom, as well as inside. The press were just finishing taking pictures, and the room was full of people. My stomach was over, and my nerves started to shake. I started rocking back and forth, because I couldn't control the emotions that were running through me.

"All rise!" The judge stepped back into the courtroom and sat down. Then the jurors came back into the room, each one sitting down slowly. Damn I can't control myself, I said to myself. There was Kim again, holding me under her arms. "We have reached a verdict on the murder charge of Famedon Young. The jury has made a wise and tough decision. When they give the verdict, I suggest everyone remain as calm as possible."

Tears rolled down my left cheek.

After all, the tears and stressing caused us to have a smaller circle. Just because you've been down with someone for years, doesn't mean their loyalty is real. Always remember you could be looking at your enemy. Everything started moving in slow motion again, while my heartbeat started racing. A juror stood up, and I heard in slow motion, "We find the defendant NOT GUILTY!" My heart jumped, because I couldn't believe what I'd heard. Not Guilty repeatedly played in my head over and over again. "Not Guilty of the murder of Famedon Young." I smiled, as the last tear poured down my face.

"We the jury find the defendant Not Guilty of 2nd Degree Murder." My heart skipped a beat, as I looked at Kim with tears in my eyes. She smiled and held me tight. Kareem smacked both hands together, squeezing tightly together, while tears poured down. Reggie smiled, putting his hands over his head and rocking back and forth. He too let tears pour down his face. As for Ra, he finally had the chance to turn around and look at me. He looked at me with tears in his eyes, then winked at me. Welcome, home Ra! We did it, I thought to myself. Thank you, God.

CHAPTER 22

"Come on babe, we are going to be late," I said to Ra, as I was putting on my dress. It was Kim and Kareem's baby shower/ wedding, and we were getting ready to go. At least that is what I thought. "We late RA!" I yelled out to him. Of course, he ignored me and still procrastinated to get out of the bed. It's been four months since Ra came home, and it's been such a blessing. We had gone on our trip to the Bahamas for 2 weeks, the week after he came home. Kareem, Kim, and Reggie came along as well. It had been the coldest winter without him and a blasting summer with him. It really feels good to have him home.

Today was our best friends shower. Kim was due in 2 weeks now, and I couldn't wait until my niece Kyra came along., Of course, I planned Kim and Kareem's shower/ wedding at The Loe Boathouse at Central Park. It was an indoor and outdoor ceremony. Outdoors would be the wedding, and indoors was the baby shower. The set up was nice as they walked down the aisle.

Since they were having a girl, I used cotton candy and pink colored balloons and accessories. The cake I ordered for the baby shower was combined with a wedding cake. A baby coming out of the bag, catching a bouquet. I had baby shaped faces as cupcakes, and a diamond ring in a box as a cake as well. I knew Kim would love my idea. It was such a cute theme.

"Babe come on we have to make it there before Kim and Kareem. You know Kim is the bride, and she doesn't want anybody seeing her." I planned Kim's wedding myself. I was her bridesmaid and Ra was Kareem's best man. Of course, Ra does what he wants and doesn't listen to me. He continued to play around as I told him to get up. Ra started kissing on my neck, and I pushed him away.

"Ra, you know we became born again Christians, so we cannot behave in the same manner anymore." Since Ra came home and we've become born again Christians, we've given our lives to Christ. God is now our "Lord and Savior" and the head of our household. We are now active church members, who go to church faithfully. We also attend church functions, as well as participate in bible study. This experience has taught us a lot. It showed us that we could not make it in this world alone, but only by keeping and putting God first throughout everything. As well as repenting for the sins that have taken place in our lives. This has made our faith strong as well as our relationship. I look forward to what God has in store for us and I'm excited to be a part of it. Kim and Kareem also attend the same church service together.

We decided to stay celibate until marriage. We slipped up a couple of times since he came home, but decided not to be intimate until marriage. Even though it is hard for the both of us, we are able to trust God through this.

"Yes, you are right and I apologize Lord, and to you Tye as well. But I love you and want to spend the rest of my life with you." "Aww! Babe, I love you too." "I want to spend the rest of my life with you too," I said, kissing him on the lips. "Tye close your eyes," he said. "Dang babe gifts already?" I asked, closing my eyes with a grin on my face. "Now open them," he said. As I slowly opened my eyes, I saw a red box. The box laid on his chest. "Aww, babe… really? For me?" I asked, smiling without another word and opened the box.

To my surprise, there sat an elegant, custom-cut yellow diamond, that was encircled by a double row of bead set, white diamond engagement ring.

I put my hands over my mouth in complete shock. "What babe?" "What is this?" I asked, staring at the ring. "Duh, it's a ring!" We both started cracking up. "No seriously babe?" "Tye! I can't explain how thankful I am to have you by my side. How you stay by my side whether I'm wrong and right. You never gave up on me, and I need someone like you forever in my life. I want to really make you Mrs. Right. I want the pleasure of having you for a lifetime and being my wife." He got out of the bed and got on one knee and asked, "WILL YOU MARRY ME?"

I was so shocked because I wasn't expecting this at all, but I wasn't stupid to say no. "Yessss... I'll marry you" I said, with eyes full of tears. Ra took the ring out of the box and placed it on my ring finger. I pulled back to see how beautiful it was, then looked at how handsome he was. I gave him another kiss on the lips and said, "this means I have to start planning." I guess sooner than later we will be intimate, I thought to myself. "All we had to do was trust God." I said smiling.

I jumped off the bed and proceeded to prepare myself for Kim and Kareem's wedding/ baby shower. "You stuck with me now," I said to him, while running in the bathroom. I was excited and wanted to tell Kim but, this was her day, so I would try and wait until later. I looked in the mirror and said, "thank you, God, for everything you have done. You've made every way possible, and I know you will be able to help us along the way. Without you, this would not be a dream come true. I will continue to walk by faith and not by sight." When the mirrors got fogged up, I jumped in the shower.

We arrived just in time for Kim and Kareem's wedding/ shower. Like I imagined it to be, it was perfect. A good enough crowd and beautiful weather. The guests were outside, as well as inside admiring everything. "Babe wow! It's so beautiful" I said looking around. Being that it was the middle of October, the weather was actually beautiful. "Good, we made it before Kim and Kareem," Ra said smiling. I couldn't help but laugh. I was just in a good mood and feeling so blessed. Especially with my new fiancé. Today was going to be a good, day, I thought to myself.

I noticed Kim and Kareem pulling up, and I didn't know what was going on. I jumped out of the car to greet them. "Babe park the car," I said and kissed him. "Ok fiancée," he said, as I got out the car. I smiled back at him. "I LOVE YOU!" I said, as I slammed the door and he drove off. "Girl why you not dressed? Kareem can't see you now." I said, rushing over to her. "Girl! Help me get into the dress, I can't even put the dress on. I feel so big," I laughed. Kim wasn't even dressed nor was Kareem. "Girl you know you late, we been here waiting for you," I said, trying to make it seem like I was early.

"Tye! Don't start, I know your ass just got here." Kim said. We busted out and started laughing. "You are not slick," Kareem said. "I was texting your fiancé," Kareem said laughing. "Yesss! Girl we heard. Congratulations!" Kim said hugging me. "You guys knew?" I asked, hugging Kim with a smile on my face. "Yeah girl, we went with him to pick out the ring, while you were so busy getting my wedding/ baby shower together." "Aww wow really," I said smiling. "Nice ring babe!" Kim said. "Thank, Kim, thanks Kareem... Aww," I said, feeling the love.

As we all were in our glory, we almost forgot about the ceremony that was supposed to take place. Being that we were really late, we had to rush inside to get Kim dressed. The guests were already preoccupied with some desserts and champagne. I had ordered a band to play good music as well. "Ok girl lets go... come Kareem," Kim said. "Where is Ra? It shouldn't take that long for him to park a car," Kareem said.

"Yes, I know," I said to myself. I reached in my purse and called him, but he didn't answer. "He probably can't find parking," Kim said. "Yeah, but it still should not take this long for parking Kim," I said looking at her.

Kareem started calling him, and he wasn't getting an answer either. "Kim go inside and get dressed. I'll meet you there. Let Keisha start on your make up." I told her, and Kim wobbled along. "Kareem I'm going to check around the corner to see if he's over there." "I'm going to go with you," he said. Before we could even get to the corner, we noticed a few people running. I had a strange look on my face, because I didn't know why they were running. I then heard sounds coming from around the corner. They sounded like firecrackers, but I knew what sound that was. I looked at Kareem. He dropped everything and ran towards the shots…

As he ran, people were running in our direction, and I knew it couldn't be good. "They are shooting a car up!" a lady yelled, and my heart dropped to my stomach. "Oh no… Ra," I said to myself and took my shoes off and ran towards the corner. For some reason, I was running in slow motion. Like something or someone was pulling me back. But my heart kept pulling me forward. I already heard the sirens around the corner, but it took me forever to reach around the corner. As I arrived around the corner, all I saw were cops, ambulances, and people around. I didn't even notice Kareem, until I saw him sitting on the ground.

My surroundings moved slowly, and I couldn't even hear myself think. My vision became blurry as I saw Ra's car door wide open and a couple of shots in the car. I kept on running, but still, I was being weighed down. As I reached near Ra's car, Kareem jumped up holding me. I couldn't speak nor hear what he had to say. I was deaf at this point, and I was blind. I wanted to see Ra, but I couldn't see him.

My heart started beating faster and all the air in my body released. I started feeling my chest close in again, and at this point, I wanted to go as well. "Raaa!" I yelled out, but I couldn't hear myself speak. "Raaa! Raaa!" I screamed and screamed out several times, as if I was talking to myself. I know people looked at me like I was crazy, but I didn't even care. As I screamed out his name some more, my voice cracked, which caused me to cough.

Kareem was still holding me, while I was still pulling towards Ra, but I couldn't get to him. "Raaa! You hear me talking to you?" I asked not hearing myself. I was getting so angry. My vision was in a complete blur, and I couldn't notice my surroundings. "Raaaaaaaaa! RAAAA!" I said louder and louder, and still, no Ra came out of the car. I dropped to the ground with Kareem trying to hold me up, but he couldn't. I laid on the ground breathing hard. Not a single tear fell down.

At this point, I felt my pain, and I heard voices. I saw people, and I saw blood. Then my anxiety turned into tears. I felt myself crying not seeing the car that sat in front of me. At this point, everything around me was a BLURR.... Nothing around me made sense. I was beginning to lose my mind. And my strength started to get weak.

The cramp in my stomach hurt like a knife was being inserted. All I could do was hold myself, while laying on the ground calling out "Raaa!" I then felt the blackness in my eyes, as if I were fading away. I couldn't see anymore, and I passed out yelling "Raaa!!", holding my cramped stomach...

"Raaa!!!!!!" I scream out....... This time I zoned out...

35209616R00077

Made in the USA
Lexington, KY
02 April 2019